ADAM GOODMAN

A Golden Orb Publication

First published 2012

For further information email –

info@goldenorbpublications.com

Hardback ISBN 978-0-9570324-0-8
Paperback ISBN 978-0-9570324-1-5

Printed by Dorman & Sons Ltd
Artwork by Darren R. Nash

www.kingcool.tv

www.goldenorbpublications.com

CONTENTS

Chapters

Illustrations

PREFACE

The story of 'King Cool' is written in the literary style of a screenplay. This writing format enables you to develop your own unique and innovative personal interpretation of the King Cool story. It is a story-telling style that has stood the test of time from epic works such as Shakespeare ... up until today, when all movies, plays and musicals use this classic format.

It allows the reader to view the King Cool story with the creative eyes and perspective of a movie director or actor. Location, time of day and character development are indicated at the beginning of each act or scene. Plot directives are sometimes briefly punctuated through the scene to act as a guide as the story unfolds. The words or dialogue of each character appear under their name. Sometimes a tone of music may be suggested to further enhance the background mood woven through a scene. For those readers used to traditional book structures, the King Cool story is also presented in chapters.

There are various scene descriptions and abbreviations that denote different action changes. They are as follows -

EXT.	- Exterior location
INT.	- Interior location
PIC.	- Picture / image
CAMERA	- Denotes the action or movement from the viewpoint of the reader or viewer.
PAN	- Camera / image moves left or right, up or down.
ZOOM IN	- Camera / image moves closer to the subject.
ZOOM OUT	- Camera / image pulls back from the subject.
FADE TO BLACK	- Picture slowly disappears to black.
FADE UP	- Picture / sound slowly appears / gets louder.
CUT TO	- Picture / image quickly moves to next image.
MIX TO	- Picture / image merges together into next image.

This is also an innovative format for people who enjoy reading stories to children. So feel free to indulge your creative imagination as you explore the amazing experiences of King Cool.

MAIN CHARACTERS

The President
Abbas O'Banna

King Finn MacCool

Hugh MacCool

Queen Suraya
Wife of King Finn MacCool

Soby
Son of Big Yin

The Big Yin

The TV Challenge

1

ACT 1.

BLACK SCREEN

Music begins to fade up. The tone is quietly tense with a distinctive 'New World Celtic Fusion' rhythm. The tension builds with a lush, mysterious and intriguing intensity.

FADE UP PIC:

EXT. SEASHORE - EVENING

The scene opens on a close-up of surging waves crashing against unusual hexagonal rock shapes. As music builds CAMERA pulls back to reveal awesome and surreal hexagonal rock columns which glow like gold, lit by a spectacular sunset as they reach up into a darkening dusk sky.

A montage of images start to show intriguing rock shapes, and dramatically lit seascapes. Fast cut, almost subliminal pictures start to be introduced between rock and sea scape images. They look like old drawings or litho-prints that build up to show a mythical, giant like human form. He is dressed in ancient medieval period clothes. We see brief images of ordinary people gazing at the huge scale of the figure. Their faces are stricken with awe and amazement.

CAMERA begins to rise up above dramatic hexagonal rock shapes. As it gets higher and higher, it starts to reveal a grid-like pattern in the rocks. This image begins to fuse and morph into the blurred pattern created on a digitized TV screen.

During this image transition, the music changes to a pulsating rock song. As the blurred picture gradually comes into focus, we begin to recognize the outline of an american prime time TV chat-show studio set. CAMERA zooms in towards the famous Rock Star, Jono James, belting out his latest hit to a live TV audience. He comes from Ireland, is in his mid-forties, has longish brown hair and wears dark glasses. He is small in stature but is big in on-stage personality with a voice to match. When the singer finishes his song, the audience stand up cheering and applauding wildly.

The singer then walks across the set to be greeted by famous female TV chat-show host - Offra Whitney.

She is an assertive middle aged Afro-American chat show legend with a huge TV audience and following world-wide. She gets up from a studio sofa to applaud the Rock Star and address the audience.

INT. TV STUDIO - EVENING

TV HOST
Ladies and gentlemen... did I not tell you... this could be our greatest ever show...

Audience applaud and scream enthusiastically.

TV HOST
Wow! ...The guests we have here tonight...

Rock Star embraces the TV host. Eventually the audience calms and they sit on the sofa.

TV HOST
Jono that was just rockin'... there's no doubt about it... you simply... are the man!

ROCK STAR
Thank you Offra, you're very kind... wow... what a show and what an audience.

Audience react by cheering, clapping and screaming.

TV HOST
Oh my... this man really is the 'King of Rock'.

ROCK STAR
Oh hold on there... I think that's going a bit far.

TV HOST
Listen to these people... they love you... come on Jono... you're today's Rock King.

ROCK STAR
Oh well, if you say so Offra.

Audience applauds excitedly.

TV HOST

Well I said this was going to be a very special show... and they don't come any more special than my final guest this evening. They certainly don't get any bigger... that's for sure. Ladies and gentlemen... it is an honour to welcome to my show a very good friend... who also just happens to be... the President of the United States of America.

Studio music strikes up 'Hail to the Chief'. Audience goes delirious with excitement as President Abbas (Baz) Obanna comes on stage. He is a tall, middle aged, well groomed Afro-American. Audience rise to applaud him. He waves to audience and then goes to join the TV host and Rock Star who are standing to applaud him.

PRESIDENT

Thank you Offra... thank you so much.

They embrace. The President then reaches over, shakes the Rock Star by the hand and then they embrace with a manly hug.

TV HOST

I guess you two are old buddies by now.

PRESIDENT

We sure are Offra.

They all sit down.

PRESIDENT

Jono and I share a lot in common... not just in music... but the state that the world is in right now... we both want to see change... and nowhere is this needed more, than in Africa. Jono, as you all know, has done just fantastic humanitarian work... not just in Africa but all over the world. He is one of my all time heroes.

Audience cheers and applauds. The Rock Star acknowledges the audience. The President continues.

PRESIDENT

...And he was kind enough to play for me... with his band... at my Presidential inauguration.

ROCK STAR

What a great honour and privilege that was for us to play for the President. This was a man whom I believed could bring about real change... not just in America... but across the world.

Audience applauds and cheers.

TV HOST

And this is in fact, the reason why both of you very important personalities in the world... have joined us here today. It's part of a very special initiative which you are launching... and is in fact... something that is very close to the hearts of the three of us... namely the continuing plight of our brothers and sisters in Africa. After years of confronting disease, poverty, wars and corruption... and despite the many and various aide programmes for that continent... the situation in Africa just isn't getting any better. So together we are seeking to set up... 'Arena for Africa'... a special forum that will seek to finally get to grips with the continuing chaos in Africa.

ROCK STAR

That's right Offra... like yourself, I've been involved with projects to help Africa for many years now... but to-date we haven't been able to crack the endemic problems ingrained in the political structures in Africa.

PRESIDENT

That's exactly it. As most people know my father was born in Kenya... so 'Arena for Africa'... takes on a very special importance for me. This is our attempt to break that history of failure... and try to build a platform of stability... for all Africans to move forward. It's not going to be easy. God knows... in this my first term in office... things haven't exactly been easy in our own country of the United States. As everyone in the audience is well aware... trying to get to grips with all of our own problems... has been slow and problematical. Every time you try to progress... something or someone comes out of the wood-work to stymie your initiative...

President gives a sigh of frustration and despair.

PRESIDENT

...Sometimes I feel it's going to take something more than time, to somehow shake up our political structures... and to solve our problems... not just in this country... but around the world.

The TV host suddenly responds sounding somewhat surprised by the President's remark.

TV HOST

What are you saying Mr. President! You sound more than a little frustrated. Excuse me... but are you not... the President? Do you not have the power to change things?

The President starts to look a little uncomfortable and looks cautiously at the TV host.

PRESIDENT

Well as President... I'm beginning to understand that some of our problems here in America... like in Africa...

(MORE)

PRESIDENT (cont'd)
are ingrained in the system... and the culture that has grown up around that system...

TV host interrupts.

TV HOST
For a man who is currently seeking his re-election for a second term in office... you suddenly are not sounding so optimistic about what can be achieved.

The President's mood suddenly becomes more upbeat as he tries to redress his initial negative comments.

PRESIDENT
And that is exactly why... you do need more time. So that's why... I need all your support at the forth-coming election... to ensure a second term in office as your President. I know we really can turn things around... and make that change.

Audience stand up, shout and applaud wildly in approval.

TV HOST
Thank goodness for that... I thought for a moment that your crown as the 'King of Cool' was starting to slip a little.

PRESIDENT
'King of cool?'... I don't know about that.

TV HOST
Oh - come on Baz... sorry... I mean... Mr. President... you know that wherever you go in the world... you're seen as the ultimate... 'King of Cool'.

The Rock Star interrupts.

ROCK STAR
But not the original 'King of Cool'...

TV HOST
The original king of cool? I'm sorry... but I would say that... worldwide, this man is definitely high on the list as one of the... the original 'Kings of Cool'.

PRESIDENT
Hold on there Offra, I think there are a lot more deserving cool dudes... who could claim that title!

TV HOST
OK... like name one?

PRESIDENT
Oh there's lots. For me... Martin Luther King... Sidney Pottier... and what about the very original... Mr. Nat... King Cool!

ROCK STAR
Nat King Cool! I like that... God you're funny as well as cool.

TV HOST
I'm sorry Baz, when it comes to the global profile... you are definitely the first 'King of Cool' across the planet.

The Rock Star interrupts.

ROCK STAR
I'm sorry but I have to disagree with you Offra... on a sort of technical time point. You see... the President is not exactly the first or original 'King of Cool'.

TV HOST
He's not? Then tell me who is?

The Rock Star's mid Atlantic accent starts to take on a more distinctive Irish brogue.

ROCK STAR

Ah well now... you're hardly going to be surprised to find out... that the original 'King of Cool'... was in fact... Irish!

The President, TV host and audience burst into spontaneous laughter.

TV HOST

God Jono... you are also a very funny man.

ROCK STAR

No... I'm absolutely serious. ...The very first King of Cool... was not only cool... and not only Irish, but he really was a bona fide... ruler and king.

The President speaks trying not to laugh.

PRESIDENT

Tell me... I must know his name.

ROCK STAR

His name... surprisingly enough... was... King... MacCool.

Everyone again bursts out laughing. The Rock Star continues.

ROCK STAR

In fact to give him his full title... he was... King Finn MacCool.

Audience laughs again.

ROCK STAR

He was a big man... very tall... a bit like yourself Mr. President... in fact you could have been related to him.

Audience laughs.

ROCK STAR

Finn MacCool was a real giant of a man... in fact... his absolutely full title was - The Giant, King Finn MacCool.

Audience breaks into uncontrolled laughter. TV host tries to wipe away tears of laughter from her eyes.

TV HOST
Oh, this story just gets better. God you Irish really have the gift of the gab.

ROCK STAR
But this is a true story... believe me.

PRESIDENT
Maybe I am related to him... you know I am in fact part Irish on my mother's side.

ROCK STAR
There you go... so you could be related! Anyway Mr. President... you keep promising me that you'll come over to Ireland to experience some Irish hospitality... and you can even look up your distant Irish relatives. You never know... you might even be related... to the original 'King of Cool'.

TV HOST
The giant!

ROCK STAR
...The giant.

Everyone laughs again.

ROCK STAR
Come on Mr. President... it's time you checked out your Irish roots... Kunta O'McKinty... and all that.

PRESIDENT
Well as you know Jono... I've had quite a bit on my plate over recent times... but to be honest I've been putting off that visit to Ireland for too long now... I might just take you up on that offer!

ROCK STAR

All right!

The President and the Rock Star high five.

ROCK STAR

Is that a definite?

PRESIDENT

You have my word. As you know with an election to fight... I've a very busy schedule... but why not... let's make it one of those quick surprise visits.

TV HOST

Well I'm going to let you two get on with making arrangements to visit the 'old country'. I hope you both come back and tell us all about your encounter with the original... and first... 'King of Cool'... from Ireland !

Audience cheers and applauds. TV host speaks over the cheering crowd.

TV HOST

Ladies and gentlemen... what a show... what a show! It just leaves me on behalf of everyone privileged to be here today... to thank these two amazing gentlemen.

Wild applause and cheers from audience.

TV HOST

Mr. President... Jono... we wish you well with your fantastic efforts with the 'Arena for Africa Forum'... I will certainly be there... and Mr. President... we wish you well in your campaign to be re-elected for a second term.

Audience stands up cheering and applauding.

TV HOST

It just leaves me to say thank you to everyone... what a great audience you've been... and how can I possibly follow this show next time... thank you all... goodbye.

The President and Rock Star get up from the sofa and wave to the audience. Excitement reaches a crescendo as they exit the stage. Music and cheering start to fade.

FADE TO BLACK.

INT. TV STUDIO DRESSING ROOM - EVENING

Pic mixes up to reveal a dressing room in the TV studio. Wife of the President and First Lady, Rachel Obanna, is waiting for her husband to come off stage. She is a tall, well-groomed, middle-aged Afro-American woman. She paces up and down in a somewhat agitated manner. A middle-aged white man is calmly lying back on a sofa watching a TV monitor, which has a live link to the TV studio floor. He is Ruben Kissenberg, the President's most senior election campaign manager. The dressing room door bursts open. Two secret service agents enter the room and look around. They stand at the door as the President enters followed by two of his personal aides - George, a well groomed Afro - American college graduate in his early thirties and Lucy, a small, rather quiet but efficient PA. She is in her mid-twenties, fair skinned with natural blond hair.

BODYGUARD 1

Everything is good Mr. President!

PRESIDENT

Thank you Bob.

The bodyguards leave the room and the President moves towards an empty sofa.

PRESIDENT

Wow... I'm glad that's over... boy the things I get myself into.

He flops down on the sofa sounding exhausted. Lucy brings the President a drink. The First Lady is still pacing.

PRESIDENT
Well... what did you think?

The First Lady can hold back her frustration no longer and suddenly lets fly at the President.

FIRST LADY
Let me tell you what I think. On top of a crazy election schedule - which means your family rarely sees you any more... you're getting more exhausted everyday and rapidly burning yourself out... so now you suddenly decide to add an overseas trip to Ireland, just before the election! It's just mad... you're committing electoral suicide!

The President suddenly sits up on the sofa.

PRESIDENT
Wooh!... Hold on there Rachel... I don't need this at the moment. What was I to do? It was one of those spur of the moment things.

FIRST LADY
You seem to be having a lot of those of late.

PRESIDENT
Look... you know I've been promising Jono to visit him in Ireland for ages now... I owe him one! Come on Ruben, help me out here.

Ruben quietly sits up and measures his answer.

RUBEN
Well Baz... Rachel is only looking out for you... I know she's concerned about you stressing out with our mission impossible election schedule...

Ruben turns and speaks directly to the First Lady.

RUBEN
But that's exactly it. This is the Presidential election to win a second term in office. Come on Rachel, you knew it was not going to be easy... you've been here before... four years ago.

FIRST LADY
That was different. Now, as well as fighting an election... being President means you also have to run the country... during one of the worst periods in America's history... not to mention the added burden of jetting all over the world like some global peace keeper and bank manager... can't you see, it's just too much for any one man.

First Lady goes over and sits beside the President on the sofa and puts her arm around him. She gives him a warm embrace. He affectionately responds.

PRESIDENT
I'm sorry hun'... I promise I'm going to try to make more room in the schedule for you and the girls.

FIRST LADY
And you need to get some chill time for yourself.

PRESIDENT
OK... I'll promise.

RUBEN
On the plus side... a visit to Ireland before the election may not be the worst move in the world.

GEORGE
How come Ruben?

RUBEN

Well with the polls showing this race going right down to the wire... endearing yourself to the huge Irish-American vote... could in fact prove a very smart move.

PRESIDENT

OK!

RUBEN

It can also give us a chance to re-endorse one of America's more successful foreign policy ventures in recent years when we helped broker the Good Friday Agreement between the Catholics and Protestants to resolve the troubles in Northern Ireland.

GEORGE

Good call! This may in fact turn out to be another of the President's off-the-cuff master strokes.

PRESIDENT

Maybe this one could have a bit of Irish luck attached to it. Tell me Ruben... do you think I could fit in a couple of days on the way back from the Africa Forum?

At that point a knock is heard at the door. It opens to reveal one of the bodyguards.

BODYGUARD 1

Excuse me Mr. President.

PRESIDENT

Yes Bob, what is it?

BODYGUARD 1

Mr. Jono is here and would like a word.

PRESIDENT

Sure, show him in.

The bodyguard gestures for the Rock Star to enter the room. The Rock Star enters and seems very upbeat.

ROCK STAR
Not interrupting am I?

The President gets up to shake hands with his friend.

PRESIDENT
Not at all... come on in.

The Rock Star acknowledges the others in the room and goes over to give the First Lady a friendly embrace.

PRESIDENT
We were just discussing how we can fit in our visit to Ireland.

ROCK STAR
Are you serious? You're definitely going to come?

PRESIDENT
I gave you my promise on air... so let's make it happen!

ROCK STAR
Fantastic... we're going to have a blast.

PRESIDENT
Get your people to liaise with my people and let's all go to Ireland... and have some fun.

ROCK STAR
Great!

PRESIDENT
Ruben thinks maybe we can fit it in on the way back from the Africa Forum.

RUBEN
I'll check it out and see what's possible.

PRESIDENT
By the way Ruben... do you think you can trace some of my relatives in Ireland. If we can arrange a meeting with them... it could provide a good photo op.

The President turns to the Rock Star.

PRESIDENT
And I wouldn't mind meeting this King Cool guy... he sounds awesome.

ROCK STAR
Ah... that may prove a little difficult.

PRESIDENT
Why is that?

ROCK STAR
Well... he was supposed to live in Ireland... like, thousands of years ago.

PRESIDENT
Supposed to live? Is this another one of your blarney stories?

ROCK STAR
No way... no, no... he's for real... he's a legend there... in Ireland... really famous... a giant of a man!

PRESIDENT
So you've told us... I can't wait... let's make this happen. And perhaps we can find time to relax a bit before coming back for the final election push... Maybe I can get a chance to sample some of that famous Irish hospitality.

ROCK STAR
I'm your man.

President turns to Ruben.

PRESIDENT

So let's keep the ceremonial elements of the visit to a minimum. Make it sound more like a social call this time to see friends and family. Do you know... I think this is one trip, I'm really looking forward to.

FADE TO BLACK.

The 'Craic' Dealers

2

Fade up contemporary, etherial Irish music. Pic fades up to reveal the President's Airforce One in flight. This is followed by a montage of images in Ireland including green fields, mountains, lakes and famous landmarks etc. It finishes with dramatic images of the strange hexagonal stones at the Giant's Causeway World Heritage site in Northern Ireland.

These images then merge into a montage of pics showing the President and the First Lady arriving in Ireland, shaking hands with crowds of people waving Irish and American flags. Pics and music slowly fade.

The mood changes as lively traditional Irish fiddle music pierces the darkness. Pic fades up to reveal the exterior of a quaint Irish Inn at the village of Bushmills in County Antrim, which is very near to the famous Giant's Causeway, in the most northerly part of Ireland. It is evening time and the street is relatively empty except for the presence of some fairly obvious United States Secret Service agents guarding the building. The music can be heard coming from the Inn. The CAMERA zooms in towards the front door and then mixes to the interior of the beautiful old country pub.

The CAMERA tracks towards the President who is sitting with the First Lady and PA's George and Lucy, grouped around a cosy turf fire in the Resident's Lounge having drinks. They are dressed in casual clothes, relaxing after a successful but tiring visit to Africa and a rapturous reception from the people of Ireland. They are now taking some time out before returning to America. The Rock Star, Jono, has fulfilled the President's request to visit the Giant's Causeway where legend has it, the original 'King of Cool' - King Finn MacCool, once ruled.

INT. VILLAGE INN RESIDENTS LOUNGE - EVENING

PRESIDENT
Well now... isn't this the life?

GEORGE
This is definitely different to a Friday night
in Washington DC.

Lucy is relaxing on an old rocking chair and sounding a bit dreamy.

LUCY
It's a different world.

First Lady turns to the President.

FIRST LADY
I know... originally... I was against this trip... but I haven't seen you this much at ease with yourself for months. ...I think our visit to Ireland has definitely agreed with you.

The President sits back and relishes another drink from his pint of Guinness.

PRESIDENT
What more could you want... great hospitality, great friends...
(He looks at the First Lady)
...and a great family.

FIRST LADY
That unfortunately is the one down side... we're going to miss Hallowe'en at home with the girls ... but when I tell them how relaxed you are... I know they'll forgive us.

PRESIDENT
What a pity Jono had a gig on tonight... he never disappoints his fans. However, we've him to thank for arranging our visit here... but we'll have to discover the whereabouts... of this 'King of Cool' guy for ourselves tomorrow.

LUCY
Where are we tomorrow?

GEORGE
Well we're going to see this King of Cool's most famous landmark at this... Giant's Causeway.

LUCY
Oh... sounds exciting.

FIRST LADY
What exactly is it?

GEORGE
Well it's listed as a World Heritage site and is supposed to be one of the natural wonders of the world.

FIRST LADY
Sounds impressive.

GEORGE
Apparently it is made up of thousands of these huge hexagonal columns of rock which were naturally formed millions of years ago... and they are all joined together to form a roadway that stretches out from the land into the sea.

PRESIDENT
But according to local myth and legend... this was actually at one time... a great and spectacular land bridge that this King of Cool guy built across the Irish Sea to Scotland.

LUCY
So what happened to it?

PRESIDENT
Well I'm not too sure. ...There's something about a great battle that took place on the Causeway between this King of Cool and some warring Scottish Chieftain when it all got destroyed.

FIRST LADY
There always has to be a war...

PRESIDENT
I'd really like to know more about it. Maybe some of the locals can help fill me in with the story.

The President finishes off his pint. Lucy gets up to get him a drink.

LUCY

Another pint Mr. President? I'll get the waiter.

The President gets up and gestures Lucy to sit down.

PRESIDENT

No, no... you all take it easy ...this round is on me!... Come on, what are we all having?

The President takes their drinks orders. He then speaks to his bodyguards at the door who follow him into the main bar area. The bar is busy and full of people dressed-up in Hallowe'en fancy dress costumes. The President's bodyguards get anxious as they try to blend into the crowd. The President goes up to the bar counter and stands beside two large men who are dressed in fluorescent yellow one-piece skeleton outfits. They are drinking pints of beer and are already well into the Hallowe'en spirit.

SKELETON 1

What about ye' big lad... can ye' give us a bit o' yer' craic.

(Pronounced crack)

The President is taken aback and looks concerned because he thinks the man has asked him for some crack cocaine.

PRESIDENT

Oh no... sorry... I definitely stay away from that stuff.

The two locals look perplexed and bemused.

SKELETON 1

Oh right... please yourself... I was only trying to be civil.

SKELETON 2

Maybe with that serious look on your face... you don't have any craic.

PRESIDENT
Excuse me... but I'm not exactly from these parts.

One of the locals answers with an ironic tone.

SKELETON 2
You're not? Now there's a surprise. God, I would have bet me house on it that you were a local.

PRESIDENT
If you don't mind me asking... what exactly do you understand as being 'crack'?

SKELETON 1
Oh you're definitely not local. Come on... stop lookin' so worried. We're only winding you up. Sure craic... is like... a sort of banter.

PRESIDENT
Banter?

SKELETON 2
It's like a social networking thing... a sort of vintage Irish twitter.

PRESIDENT
Oh crack... it's like conversation?

SKELETON 1
Well it's like conversation... but there's a lot more slaggin' off with it.

PRESIDENT
I'm not even going to go there. But if that's what crack is... I've got lots of it.

SKELETON 1
Sure everybody's got a bit o' craic... good lad.

SKELETON 2
So what are you doing here big man?

The President gestures for the two locals to come closer.

PRESIDENT
Well to tell you the truth... I'm here to see... this King of Cool guy.

The two men look somewhat quizzical and both reply in tandem.

SKELETON 1
Who?

SKELETON 2
Who?

PRESIDENT
You know... this King of Cool guy... he's supposed to be a legend around here. Do you know him?... Big guy... apparently you can't miss him!

The two locals look at each other and burst out laughing.

SKELETON 2
Come off it, now you're takin' a hand out of us.

PRESIDENT
No... I'm serious!

SKELETON 1
Man dear... you don't mean Finn MacCool... the giant?

PRESIDENT
That's the very man... the giant... King Finn MacCool.

The two locals burst out laughing again.

SKELETON 1
Well we know him... but we're not exactly personal pals like...

PRESIDENT
Oh that's too bad... I was hoping you might know something about him. ...Do you know anybody around here who does know of him?

SKELETON 2
Well if you want to know anything about Finn MacCool... there's only one man in the village you need to talk to.

PRESIDENT
Who's that?

SKELETON 1
You'd be talking about Hugh. He's a night watchman down at the local distillery.

SKELETON 2
But you have to be warned...

He puts his hand on the President's arm.

SKELETON 2
Hugh is not exactly like other men.

PRESIDENT
He's not?

SKELETON 1
No... Hugh is sort of an eccentric... a bit of a 'one off' is our Hugh.

SKELETON 2
Some say... he may even be a distant relative of King Finn MacCool himself.

The President starts to get excited.

PRESIDENT
He sounds like the very man I need to meet. Can you tell me where he lives?

SKELETON 1
Just down at the old stone gate lodge at the entrance to the distillery...

SKELETON 2
...Down at the bottom of the village.

PRESIDENT
Great... I'll go and see him in the morning.

SKELETON 2
Oh! You won't be able to do that!

PRESIDENT
Why not?

SKELETON 2
Hugh does the night shift... so he sleeps all day.

SKELETON 1
If you want to see Hugh... you better go and see him now.

PRESIDENT
I can't go now!

SKELETON 2
Why not?

PRESIDENT
Oh... they'd never let me go out at night around these parts... security risk you know.

SKELETON 1
Oh right!

SKELETON 2
Well, at night is the only time to see Hugh... and... you better go on your own. Hugh can go a bit crazy... if there's too many strangers around.

SKELETON 1
That's right... if you want to see Hugh
tonight... you better go on your own.

PRESIDENT
Oh they definitely would never let me out
on my own!

SKELETON 2
Is that right? - I think I can understand
why!

The President thinks to himself for a moment. Then he beckons the two locals to get close to him and whispers to them.

PRESIDENT
Excuse me... but would you two gentlemen
like to join me for a moment in the...
gentlemen's rest-rooms?

The two locals look at each other somewhat taken aback.

PRESIDENT
Sorry... the toilets... I mean the men's
toilets. ... Would you two gentlemen like to
meet me in the men's toilets?

The President winks knowingly at each of them. The two locals suddenly react with surprise and anger.

SKELETON 1
Now hold on a minute pal... there's craic...
and there's crack.

SKELETON 2
I'm afraid us local guys... are a bit behind
the times here in that respect... not like
you American guys.

SKELETON 1
Oh aye... what he said... if you're in'te
that sort of thing.

He beckons the President to come close to him.

SKELETON 1
You might want to have a word with Brian... he's the local ladies' hairdresser.

SKELETON 2
That's right... as far as we know...

SKELETON 1
Brian's the only gay in the village!

The President steps back in surprise.

PRESIDENT
No, no... wait a minute... it's nothing like that... no way.

He gestures to them to come closer.

PRESIDENT
Look... come here... I've got this plan...

FADE TO BLACK.

Date with Destiny

3

Pic fades up to show exterior of the Inn. It is dark and windy. The sound of the pub revelry spills out onto the empty street. Suddenly a dark figure is seen to creep out of the shadows. Its silhouette is briefly caught in the glimmer of the subdued street lights. It reveals the outline of a somewhat garish florescent day-glow yellow skeleton as it creeps along the side of the houses on the village street. The skeleton disappears into the gloom.

It is seen to re-emerge creeping up a dark country lane. It slinks past a sign which reads: 'Bushmills - The Oldest Whiskey Distillery in the World'. Eventually it arrives outside an old stone cottage gate-lodge. A soft golden light can be seen coming from the window. The only sound is the wind blowing leaves around the cottage and an owl hooting faintly in the background.

Suddenly the outline of the florescent skeleton is seen to creep spider-man like up to the cottage door. The skeleton, then hesitantly and gently, raps on the cottage door. There is no response. The skeleton knocks even louder. Still no response. Finally the skeleton knocks the door with a loud thump. Out of the silence a voice is heard in a quiet local Irish accent, coming from behind the cottage door.

EXT. STONE GATE LODGE - NIGHT

HUGH
(whispers)
Who's that out there?

The skeleton figure is in fact the President who has dressed up in a Hallowe'en outfit belonging to one of the locals in the pub.

PRESIDENT
(whispers)
It's me... is that Hugh?

HUGH
(whispers)
Who's looking for Hugh?

PRESIDENT
(whispers)
I'm looking for Hugh.

Hugh thinks the President has said - I'm looking for who?

HUGH

(Speaks in a loud voice)

Hold on now... if you're not sure who you're looking for... why are you looking for me?

Close up of the President. He reaches up to scratch his head which is still covered by the skeleton mask, looking somewhat confused.

PRESIDENT

It depends on who you are?

HUGH

I'm Hugh - who are you?

PRESIDENT

Well... at the moment... I'm a florescent yellow skeleton.

HUGH

Are you dead?

PRESIDENT

I don't think so.

HUGH

You know... I really don't like talking to dead people very much.

PRESIDENT

I'm definitely not dead.

HUGH

Well how come you're a skeleton and you're not dead?

PRESIDENT

It's a long story... and involves two men in a bar.

HUGH

Who do you say you are again?

PRESIDENT

Well to tell you the truth... I'm the President.

HUGH

The President... I don't know any Presidents. ... No, wait a minute... you're not Joe Malone are you?

PRESIDENT

No, I'm not Joe Malone... who's he?

HUGH

He's a President.

PRESIDENT

He is? ...Where of?

HUGH

The local football club.

Close up of President starting to shake his head and speaks with a more frustrated tone.

PRESIDENT

No, I'm a different kind of President... I'm President of the United States of America.

Hearty laughter heard coming from behind the door.

HUGH

Ha ha... that's a good-un... and I'm Hugh Heffner... and this is the 'bunny mansion'.

PRESIDENT

Seriously... I am the President of the USA.

HUGH

Come off it... I know we get some famous people here but there's no way that the President of the United States would just like... walk up to my door, at this time of night... without being announced... or even a phone call from the White House or somethin'.

The President looks very bemused.

HUGH
Even if he was stuck for a few bottles of the special stuff, like if he was having a big party! Sorry, I don't believe you're the President - now go away!

The President starts to sound very confused and talks to himself.

PRESIDENT
God, they said this wasn't going to be easy at the pub.

He then talks to the voice behind the door again.

PRESIDENT
How can I prove to you that I am the President?

HUGH
Well you could tell me which President you are. ...Like are you George Washington?

PRESIDENT
Would that make a difference?

HUGH
It certainly would.

PRESIDENT
Why is that?

HUGH
Well George Washington never told a lie... so if you were George Washington... or even Denzel Washington for that matter... I would believe you.

PRESIDENT
Well I'm sorry to disappoint you but I'm not George Washington... and I only wish I was Denzel Washington.

HUGH

Well then go away and stop bothering me... anyway, how do I know that you are the President of America? You could be a gang of international cut-throat booze smugglers... just waiting for me to open this door, so that you can steal all our whiskey.

The President hits his forehead with the palm of his bony hand in frustration and slumps down to sit on the ground outside the door. He shakes his head. Then suddenly he jumps up to his feet and knocks the door loudly once more.

HUGH

Who's that?

PRESIDENT

Trick or treat!

HUGH

Trick or treat what?

Then the President starts to sing a rhyme.

PRESIDENT

Hallowe'en is coming... the geese are getting fat... please put a penny in the old man's hat... if you haven't got a penny... a ha'penny will do... if you haven't got a ha'penny... God bless you!

Suddenly the bar on the inside of the door is heard to move and the door is unlocked. The door opens wide and Hugh jumps out.

HUGH

Trick or treat... why did you not say that in the first place... come on in.

The President shakes his head in disbelief and makes a gesture with his hands like a magician when he completes a magic trick. They go into the cottage.

INT. STONE COTTAGE - NIGHT

HUGH

There was no need for all that stupid President stuff... sure it's Hallowe'en... come on in and sit down.

Hugh quickly ushers the President to sit down on a chair at a table in the cottage. A wood fire glows and gives a warm cosy feel to the room. The walls are surrounded with shelves full of old books and charts. Hugh suddenly comes up behind the President and shouts.

HUGH

Nuts!

The President speaks under his breath.

PRESIDENT

I never would have guessed.

He then speaks to Hugh.

PRESIDENT

Sorry, what was that?

HUGH

Do you want any nuts... for Hallowe'en?

PRESIDENT

No, it's OK.

He then speaks under his breath.

PRESIDENT

I think I've had enough nuts tonight already.

HUGH

What about a drink? Would you like a drink? I've got some very special tea for occasions just like this.

PRESIDENT

Tea? ... OK, I'll have a cup of tea.

HUGH

No problem... I'll have it in just a jiffy.

Hugh goes into the kitchen to make the tea. The President looks around at all the books and manuscripts. He gets up and walks over to look at the books. He picks one off the shelf and looks at the title. It reads 'The Legend of Finn MacCool'. The President speaks to himself.

PRESIDENT

I guess I've come to the right place.

He puts the book back and sits down again. He shouts into Hugh in the kitchen.

PRESIDENT

You've got a great book collection here... I believe you might know Finn MacCool.

Hugh suddenly bounds back into the room carrying a tray with cups and saucers which he clatters and rattles and almost spills in excitement.

HUGH

Do you know about Finn MacCool?

PRESIDENT

Not really... that's sort of why I'm here... I heard that if I wanted to hear anything about Finn MacCool... I should definitely go and talk to Hugh.

The President reaches out to shake Hugh's hand.

PRESIDENT

I'm so pleased to meet you at last. My name is Abbas... but my friends just call me Baz.

Hugh quickly responds with a warm hearty handshake.

HUGH

Pleased to meet you Baz... anybody who likes Finn MacCool is welcome here. My name is Hugh... but people just call me... Hugh.

PRESIDENT
All right Hugh.

As Hugh starts to pour out the tea, the President reaches up and takes off his skeleton head mask to reveal his face. Hugh looks at the face of the President, suddenly jumps up and screams wildly.

HUGH
Aaaaaahhhhhhhhhh!

The cups fall sprawling across the table and Hugh almost drops the teapot. In the furore he burns himself with hot tea.

HUGH
Aaaaahhhhhhhhhhh!

PRESIDENT
I'm sorry to frighten you like that. ... Look I'll go... I'm sorry, it's just the effect I have on people... when they see the President of the United States.

Hugh starts to calm down. He shakes his hands in the air trying to cool down his third degree burns.

PRESIDENT
I'm sorry to surprise you like that. Are you OK?

HUGH
No, no... it's OK... I'm fine.

Hugh starts to stutter.

HUGH
It's just... it's just that... I'm somewhat in shock.

PRESIDENT
Don't worry, it's fairly normal. ... It happens to me a lot when people see the President.

HUGH

No, no it's nothing to do with the President thing... it's you.

Hugh goes over to the President and starts to look very closely at the skin on his face. The President seems somewhat mystified and bemused.

HUGH

It's you...

Hugh starts to rub the skin on the President's face.

HUGH

I don't believe it... this is too much.

PRESIDENT

What is?

Hugh seems very shocked and flustered. He goes over to a cabinet and takes out a large bottle full of a liquid that glistens with a golden fire as the light hits it. He brings it to the table and sets up the cups and saucers. He pours out the liquid from the bottle into the cups.

HUGH

Here, drink this... I think we're going to need it.

The President looks quizzically at Hugh.

PRESIDENT

I am?

He sips from the cup and suddenly his eyes light up with delight.

PRESIDENT

What is this? ...Wow! ...It ...it's sensational.

HUGH

It's a very special brew I keep... for very special occasions... and believe me... this is a very special occasion!

PRESIDENT

It is?

He takes another sip from the cup.

PRESIDENT

Wow!

HUGH

Oh yes... this is a very, very special occasion.

PRESIDENT

What's so special about it?

HUGH

What date is this?

PRESIDENT

It's... ahhh... it's the thirty first of October.

HUGH

Exactly... the thirty first of October... Hallowe'en.

PRESIDENT

I'm sorry, I didn't realize Hallowe'en was such a big deal here in Ireland.

HUGH

This is not just any Hallowe'en... it's Hallowe'en and you're here. ...That makes it very special indeed.

PRESIDENT

It does? How come?

HUGH

This fulfils an ancient prophecy... and you're part of it!

PRESIDENT

I am?

Hugh gets quickly up from the table and goes over to the shelves of books. He runs his finger across them, dust flies up as he searches for a book. He suddenly stops.

HUGH
A-ha!

He picks an old leather bound manuscript from the shelves. He brushes the dust off it and sets it on the table beside the President. He sits down again and starts to leaf through the book.

HUGH
It's here somewhere...

The President seems somewhat bemused.

HUGH
Wait... here it is... listen to this.

Hugh starts to read from the book.

HUGH
'On the Eve of all Hallows... you'll be taken aback... when the tall man appears... who is covered in black.'

The President now looks very bemused and Hugh points at him.

HUGH
You see... covered in black... Eve of all Hallows... Hallowe'en... the one night of the year when this world... and the spirit world... are at their closest... and com'ere... there's more. ...'Then sip golden nectar... from the glass urn... to witness the wonder... of Great Finn's return.'

PRESIDENT
So what made him so great?... This Finn the cool.

Hugh looks pensively into the distance and begins to speak with emotion.

HUGH

You see King Finn MacCool, was no ordinary man... and no ordinary king. He had some very special gifts. You see, during all the time of his rule he had the amazing ability to ensure his people lived in total peace and harmony... despite there being so many war-mongering chieftains around. He would find a way to disarm his enemies through his charm and warm friendly personality... not to mention an acute sense of wit and sharpness of thought, to defuse any threatening situation. He believed we could all live happily together in a world without violence and anger... if only we set our minds to it... to overcome our own selfish desires and inner demons. As a result, all of his subjects loved him for the stability and prosperity he brought to his land... and he did it all without ever having to make war or raise his voice. ...You see he really was... the original 'King of Cool'.

PRESIDENT

Wow... with all that I'm having to deal with in the world at present... this is one man I would loved to have met.

Hugh looks down at the book again.

HUGH

Hold on... it finishes with this... 'Stand on the Great Causeway... over night skies so black... fix your gaze on dark waters... to welcome him back.'

Hugh suddenly jumps up.

HUGH

Come on... drink that up... I've got something to show you.

The President drinks back the golden liquid. By now its effects are starting to make him feel a little tipsy.

PRESIDENT
Boy... this is good stuff... Hugh, do you think you could arrange a few barrels of this gorgeous nectar to be sent to me at the White House?

Hugh comes over to the President who is pouring himself another drink from the special bottle. He knocks it back in one go.

PRESIDENT
Wow!

HUGH
Come on... you... have a legend to fulfil.

The President sets the cup down on the table and is starting to sound tipsy.

PRESIDENT
I do? ... Wow... I can't wait!

HUGH
Come on... we haven't got much time.
...Let's go!

FADE TO BLACK.

On the Rocks

4

Pic fades up to show Hugh hurrying the President outside to an old barn. They go inside, Hugh lifts off a cover to reveal an old motorbike and side-car. The opening chords of a fast tempo rock 'n' roll song begin to fade up.

INT. OLD STONE BARN - NIGHT

HUGH
Come the hour, cometh... the 'Silver Streak'! You're not nervous of speed are you Baz? This is a flying machine, she's been raced in the North West 200 you know... we'll be there in no time.

PRESIDENT
Something tells me I shouldn't be doing this!

Hugh and the President hop on board. Hugh drives. The President gets into the side-car. They put on some old fashioned crash helmets. After much noise and back firing the 'Silver Streak' fires up. They leave in a cloud of smoke. Hugh accelerates up to about 15 miles per hour.

EXT. COUNTRY ROAD - NIGHT

They proceed somewhat slowly down the road. The President makes a jibed remark poking fun at their rather pedestrian speed.

PRESIDENT
How many G's is this baby pullin' Hugh?

Hugh's gaze is fixed intently on the road ahead. As if to over exaggerate their speed, the President takes hold of his cheeks with the finger and thumb of each hand. He makes his cheeks wobble as if it was in a high speed wind tunnel test.

PRESIDENT
(Casually to Hugh)
I'm not sure I can take much more of this.

The President pretends to be thrown from side to side by the speed.

HUGH
Be brave Baz - you can do it. Just hold on.

The President casually takes out his mobile phone and calls his Personal Aide George back at the Inn. He sounds a little bit tipsy after taking Hugh's special golden brew.

PRESIDENT
Hi Georgie Boy, yoh bro - how goes it my man?

Cut to George on his mobile phone. The PA hesitantly replies.

GEORGE
M... M... Mister President... is that you? We wondered where you disappeared to. ... The Secret Service guys here are going crazy... are you all right?

Cut back to the President.

PRESIDENT
Georgie Boy, I've never felt better in my life! ... This is a great place. You know we Americans should get out more... see a lot more of the world... you know what I mean.

George replies somewhat hesitantly.

GEORGE
S... S... sure Mr. President... tell me, are you OK... you sound different... Where are you?

PRESIDENT
I'm on the Silver Streak powering my way to destiny at the Causeway of the Giants!

GEORGE
What?

PRESIDENT
Mysterious things could happen you know, it is written...

GEORGE
Don't panic Mr. President, we'll get there as soon as possible.

PRESIDENT
There's no problem Georgie Boy... forget about it, you needn't worry... I'm in safe hands. I'll see you later. Toodle pip.

President finishes phone call.

PRESIDENT
Don't panic he says - we're hardly in a state of panic Hugh are we?

Hugh stops the motor bike at a sign post which says 'Giants Causeway 2 miles'.

HUGH
Hold on Baz... I know a near cut.

Hugh turns the bike through the gate of an open field and suddenly the 'Silver Streak' gathers speed rapidly as the motorbike careers out of control downhill through a field of tall grass. The President starts to look very scared. Music tempo changes to pulsating 'Silver Streak' biker song.

PRESIDENT
OK now I'm panicking!

What follows is a hairy, scary and hilarious cross country bike ride. All sorts of skids, bumps, crashes through chicken sheds, cows, pigs, haystacks, rivers etc. The President is now terrified. Bike eventually crashes through a wooden gate and skids to a stop beside another signpost which says - 'Giant's Causeway 3 miles'. The President tries to catch his breath while pulling some grass and chicken feathers out of his crash helmet and mouth.

PRESIDENT
I...
(He spits out a feather)
I...
(He tries to spit out another feather)
...I thought that was supposed to be a short cut.

HUGH
Ah no! ... I just remembered Baz, that was a short cut to somewhere else I was just thinkin' of...

Cut to close up of the President's face. He looks very bemused and is about to say something when he stops himself with a look that says forget it, it's not worth it, don't go there. Instead, he gestures with his hand for Hugh to proceed. They set off down the road more sedately towards the Causeway.

CUT TO:

THE INTERIOR OF A SECRET SERVICE CAR - NIGHT

Two of the President's bodyguards are in the front and PA's George and Lucy are in the back. They are all looking anxious and concerned.

GEORGE
I hope we're not too late... by the sound of the President his mind seemed to be in such a confused state that anything could happen. ... Step on it Bob.

BODYGUARD 1
Oh boy... we're done for... letting the President out of our sight...

BODYGUARD 2
Totally done for!

CUT TO:

EXT. THE PRESIDENT AND HUGH ON MOTORBIKE ARRIVING AT THE GIANT'S CAUSEWAY ENTRANCE - NIGHT

A black cat runs across the road in front of Hugh driving the motorbike. He swerves to avoid hitting the cat and hits the side of the sign which says 'WELCOME TO THE GIANT'S CAUSEWAY - A NATURAL WONDER OF THE WORLD'. The sign wobbles and totters precariously before crashing to the ground in a thousand pieces.

PRESIDENT
That's it, two billion years to make and we demolish it in two seconds... Hugh, you realize you've just demolished one of the wonders of the world.

HUGH
I know, sure isn't this great fun Baz.

The motorbike is seen to wobble on down the road and fades into the darkness.

FADE TO BLACK.

A reprise of the intense and haunting music heard during the opening titles fades up. It creates a mysterious and somewhat eerie tone. Fade up dramatic pics showing landscapes of the Giant's Causeway glowing in the surreal silvery moonlight. Mix between spectacular pics of waves crashing into the dramatic rock columns which rise out of the sea. Mix to pics of the President and Hugh dismounting from the motorbike. They are silhouetted against the imposing Giant's Causeway landscape. Cut to close up of the President's face. He is looking around in awe and amazement.

EXT. ON THE ROCKS AT GIANT'S CAUSEWAY - NIGHT

PRESIDENT
Wow! This is awesome.

The President and Hugh are seen stepping over the strange rock shapes towards the sea. The place is desolate. The President and Hugh sit down on one of the rock shapes. Cut to close up of Hugh and the President. Hugh sounds a bit dejected and disappointed.

HUGH
Ah well, looks like you're not part of the legend after all Baz.

PRESIDENT
To tell you the truth, I never for a moment believed I was. ... But heck, this has been fun and sure I've met you Hugh...
(MORE)

PRESIDENT (cont'd)
you're a living legend in the MacCool family, not some old dead myth. Do you know Hugh, I've learnt so much from my trip here already... I wouldn't have missed it for the world - now come on, let's fire up the 'Silver Streak' and we'll finish that bottle you were feeding me.

The two men get up from the rocks, the President is seen to slip, wobble and steady himself on the wet stones.

HUGH
Woh! ... Hold on Baz.

PRESIDENT
I'm OK Hugh... lead on...

Hugh leads on and they begin to carefully move across the wet stones along the edge of the sea. The President is seen to slip and wobble precariously a couple of times. Finally he completely looses his balance and he screams out.

PRESIDENT
Hugh! ... Help me... ahaaaah!...

Hugh looks back and sees the President topple and fall into the water and disappear under the waves. The action cuts to a flash back of what has happened from the President's point of view. He sees an enormous hand and arm rise out of the water. A striking broad gold bracelet glistens around its wrist. The hand grabs the President around the ankles and drags him off the rocks down into the swell of the sea. Hugh runs to the spot where the President fell in. He looks down into the dark swelling depths and shouts out.

HUGH
Baz... Mr. President... oh my heavens... oh God... I'm in for it... I've killed the President of America.

Hugh remains gazing into the water and at that point the giant hand once more rises out of the water, grabs Hugh and pulls him into the swelling seas. The music reaches a crescendo of intrigue and drama. Hugh screams as he disappears into the water.

The CAMERA follows underneath the water - a stream of bubbles flow past the CAMERA lens. Through the dark and murky water, the faint outline of a large figure is just visible. It swims deeper and deeper towards a distant glowing orb of golden light. The large figure is seen in silhouette carrying under each arm the motionless bodies of the President and Hugh. They all disappear into the glowing sphere of gold, through a centre of pure white light. Music fades.

FADE TO BLACK.

EXT. ON THE ROCKS AT GIANT'S CAUSEWAY - NIGHT

The darkness is broken by flashing lights and torches seen searching across the Causeway. George, Lucy and the bodyguards are walking over the rocks. They are now joined by police and local air-sea rescue crews. A helicopter with a powerful search light arrives overhead and lights up the whole scene on the Causeway.

GEORGE
It's been over an hour now, and there's still no sign of him.

POLICEMAN 1
Are you sure he said it was here?

GEORGE
This is the 'Causeway of the Giants' ...isn't it?

POLICEMAN 1
You could say that.

A second policeman runs up to policeman 1.

POLICEMAN 2
Excuse me sir, we've found Hugh's old motorbike and sidecar... the engine is still warm.

POLICEMAN 1

They must be here somewhere!

Suddenly one of the searchers shouts from the rocks close to the water's edge.

RESCUER 1
Look, I've found something.

Everyone rushes down towards him. Rescuer holds up a mobile phone dripping with water.

LUCY
Oh my God... that's the President's personal mobile...

They all look at each other and go quiet. Concern and worry is reflected from their faces. They look into the swelling sea crashing into the rocks beside them. Sounding somewhat resigned the rescuer speaks to George and Lucy.

RESCUER 1
In the dark... these rocks are too slippy and very dangerous. For your own safety... I think we've done all we can tonight... we'll get a team of divers here first thing in the morning.

Lucy grabs George's arm for support as she breaks down and starts to cry.

POLICEMAN 1
It's not looking good...

POLICEMAN 2
And we've just had a call to say there's no sign of Hugh MacCool at his cottage.

Policeman 1 looks towards George.

POLICEMAN 1
You better alert your people in Washington.

Lucy tries to compose her emotions and quietly speaks through her sobs and tears.

LUCY
I think... we better get back to see the First Lady... God, I really don't know how we're going to break this to her.

GEORGE
Let's try to keep it vague for the moment... till we see what happens... come on...

The CAMERA pulls away from the group and pans across the Causeway with searchlights still flashing, picking up the strange and dramatic shape of the rock columns. The CAMERA tracks once more into and under the swelling sea. As we travel down into the depths, a montage of world newspaper front pages spin up through the swirling water. Headlines on newspapers read:

(1) "US PRESIDENT FEARED DEAD!"

(2) "TRAGIC DROWNING IN IRELAND OF PRESIDENT OBANNA"

(3) "TERRORIST PLOT NOT RULED OUT"

(4) "AL QUAEDA AND TALIBAN SAY - IT WASN'T US!"

(5) "DRINK AND DRUGS ABUSE NOW AT CENTRE OF INQUIRY"

(6) "MENTAL STRESS COULD HAVE CAUSED PRESIDENT'S SUICIDE!"

FADE TO BLACK.

Travelling Light

5

ACT 2.

Pic fades up to show CAMERA zooming under water towards the centre of the orb of bright golden light, and passes through it. Music reaches a crescendo as the dazzling white light fills the screen. Music starts to fade and through a very slow dissolve with a soft lighting effect, a close up shot of a closed human eyelid begins to appear. Suddenly the eyelid springs open to reveal a hazy brown eye. The eye blinks two or three times. CAMERA slowly pulls back to reveal the face of the President. He looks somewhat bewildered. He is lying on the ground. He slowly sits up and rubs his eyes as if awakening from a dream.

EXT. AN UNKNOWN LOCATION - DAYTIME

PRESIDENT
(Thinks to himself)
Oh God, ...where am I? ... Still, I'm breathing... confused, dazed... but still breathing!

The President rubs his eyes again and CAMERA cuts to an out of focus perspective from the President's point of view. His eyes begin to clear and slowly start to make out the outline of a strange but vast and dazzlingly beautiful landscape. As CAMERA pans around, it suddenly stops, as the President sees the body of Hugh lying motionless face down on the ground. He looks to be dead. The President's face grimaces.

PRESIDENT
Oh no!

The President quickly gets up and runs towards Hugh's body.

PRESIDENT
Hugh, Hugh!

He lifts Hugh up and turns him over. Hugh's eyes are closed but he has a somewhat silly grin on his face.

PRESIDENT
Oh no, Hugh , Hugh, wake up... It's my fault - I never should have...

He tries to awaken Hugh, but as he begins to see more clearly, he stops to observe the magnificence of the landscape and the intensity of the beautiful colours. He looks mesmerized by it. Suddenly Hugh speaks.

HUGH
Never have what Baz?

PRESIDENT
(He screams out)
Aaaagh! - don't do that to me Hugh... I thought you were...

HUGH
Sleeping - as soon as I fell into the water. ...That's it, passed out cold... Baz - where have you brought me to now?

The President embraces Hugh. Hugh looks bemused.

PRESIDENT
I... haven't brought you anywhere... did you not see the... ah... the ah... big guy... who brought us here?

HUGH
What big guy Baz?

PRESIDENT
The one who pulled us into the water.

HUGH
Baz, if you don't mind me saying so... is this not like some fantastic big dream we're both having - sure this place even looks like a dream.

They both look around at the amazing and beautiful landscape.

PRESIDENT
Hugh, you could be right... that was quite a cup of tea you made me and...

Suddenly another voice is heard to interrupt. It is the voice of King Cool, a huge giant of a man, over eight feet tall.

He has a youthful, almost timeless look with a strong handsome face and a warm friendly smile. His hair is long and golden. He is dressed in a white and gold tunic which reveals his strong athletic arms and legs. He stands, legs astride, towering over the President and Hugh with the poise and demeanor of a medieval warrior king. He speaks however in a soft and gentle North Antrim accent that reflects a deep strength of character and wisdom but with much humility. King Cool is looking at the President, but Hugh has his back to King Cool.

KING COOL
You're not having a dream.

HUGH
Now stop trying to confuse me Baz, first you say we could be having a dream and then you say we're not!

PRESIDENT
(Looking up at the size of King Cool and trembling)
I... I... I didn't say a word.

HUGH
Who did then?

The President, his hand shaking, points upwards. Camera tracks upwards to reveal the giant proportions of King Cool. Hugh seems unperturbed by his size as he speaks to King Cool.

HUGH
So big man... how do you know we're not having a dream then?

KING COOL
Because it's the truth... I brought you here... welcome to my world.

King Cool stretches out his enormous hand for Hugh to shake it.

HUGH
That's good enough for me.

Hugh goes to shake King Cool's hand, he suddenly stops, screams and grabs the President.

HUGH

Ahaaaah!! Holy socks Baz... do you see the size of that guy?...

KING COOL

Let me introduce ourselves. ... You are President Abbas Obanna of the United States of America... your friends call you Baz... and you are Hugh MacCool... a very good and distant relative of mine... and people just call you...

HUGH

Hugh.

PRESIDENT

Well I'll be!

KING COOL

Welcome, I am Finn...

HUGH

And I'm one of your relatives... well I'll be... as well.

PRESIDENT

I knew there was something special about you Hugh.

HUGH

(Hesitantly)

H... h... h... how are you Finn?

Hugh shakes Finn's hand.

KING COOL

Are we fully awake now?

The President eyes up the great size of King Cool.

PRESIDENT

Are we... very, very enormous?

KING COOL
Size isn't everything... but it helps.
...You're not exactly a hobbit yourself Baz.

HUGH
Especially when you want to frighten the living daylights out of someone... like me!

KING COOL
Don't be afraid Hugh - you're among friends here. ...My name is Finn MacCool... King Finn MacCool... if you want the full thing... but you can just call me Finn.
...Welcome to my kingdom - we've been expecting you!

PRESIDENT
You have? ... Well... excuse me King Finn... was this scheduled through my office or something...

KING COOL
No Baz... you don't mind if I call you Baz?

PRESIDENT
It would be a privilege.

KING COOL
And you can drop the King thing... anyway... this was arranged a long time ago... by destiny.

PRESIDENT
Destiny... I haven't used that department much to-date.

HUGH
Holy socks! ... You are the real Finn MacCool... this is just fantastic! ... Am I part of destiny as well?

KING COOL
You sure are Hugh... it's like we're all partners together in this destiny.

PRESIDENT
(In an aside to Hugh)
I'm kind'a taken by this big guy - the gentle giant type.

HUGH
Except that he actually is... a real giant.

PRESIDENT
What that big man could do in the NBA.

He jokingly makes a remark to King Cool.

PRESIDENT
Excuse me Finn... do you ever see your future in the States at all?

KING COOL
My friend, you are already in the future, - you are the future. In your time, I am now known as a distant legend of the past... something confined to folklore and myth. The truth is... in this world... I am the future, I am the past... because time here... is eternal.

The President and Hugh look at each other.

KING COOL
Yet the course of your destiny leads you to visit us from your world... a world constricted by time. And destiny has chosen you to learn some new ways that will help you... in your future.

PRESIDENT
But why us?!!

KING COOL
It is written. It is destiny. It says that one day, a seed of the great Kings of MacCool would return with a great dark skinned ruler of the past...
(MORE)

KING COOL (cont'd)
to learn new ways for the future of your world. ... It is sort of a family thing.

HUGH
A family thing.

KING COOL
Yes, it’s something your mother’s great, great, great, great several times over great grand father... arranged with... my mother.

HUGH
If it’s a family thing... that’s good enough for me.

KING COOL
Then it’s good enough for all of us... for now. ... Come on you need some rest... you’ve both had a busy day. ... Let’s go, you’re staying at my place...

King Cool looks at the President dressed in the skeleton outfit and smiles.

KING COOL
I think we might need to find you something to wear Baz!

They walk off down the road. A spectacular sunset spreads across the beautiful fairy tale valley, filled with a dazzling variety of colourful flowers, lush trees, and crystal glistening rivers and waterfalls. King Cool and Hugh start to whistle a happy tune, the President mutters to himself.

PRESIDENT
Indeed... a busy day it was... just your ordinary busy day... became a skeleton... drowned... time travelled... to a land of giants... and met my future destiny... yep... just your average ordinary day.

The President starts to whistle as well. They all disappear down the road through the stunning verdant valley landscape. Soft romantic music swells.

FADE TO BLACK.

Babysitting

6

INT. KING COOL'S CASTLE - EARLY MORNING

Pic fades up to show the President and Hugh sound asleep in a bedroom at King Cool's castle. The morning sun gently lights up the soft stone walls and the understated elegance of the regal decor. The room has an air of peace and quiet calm. Birds are singing outside the open window.

Suddenly the quietness is shattered by great earth shuddering tremors. Pounding and crashing sound heard in distance getting closer. The President and Hugh wake up with a start. They rub their eyes.

PRESIDENT
W... W... what's happening?

Hugh spots a note at the side of the bed. He starts to read it.

HUGH
Baz listen, here's a note from King Finn.

Reads out aloud.

HUGH
Dear Baz and Hugh, if you experience great earth-shuddering tremors don't be alarmed... large Scottish giant from the land across the Great Causeway will be advancing in your direction and he's looking to kill you. He's a bit of a...

The President suddenly interrupts Hugh in mid sentence.

PRESIDENT
Kill us!! Why us?

HUGH
(Hugh continues but struggles to read some of the words on the note)
He's a bit of a... psy ... psyco ...he's a bit of a cycle-path.

Hugh looks up at the President quizzically. The crashing footsteps get louder.

HUGH
This looks like another busy day Baz, hold on there's more...

Hugh starts to read again.

HUGH
Everything will be OK, I'll explain later, put on some sort of disguise so he won't recognize who you are when he arrives... P.S. ...Can you look after my baby in the next room? Good luck Finn.

PRESIDENT
Baby sitting at a time like this... the man's mad.

They go into an adjoining room and are astonished to see a huge baby cradle. Dangling out of the cradle are enormous arms and legs.

HUGH
Holy socks Baz - that's a big baby!

PRESIDENT
I don't know what they feed them on around here, but I must get some.

All the time the sound of the crashing footsteps are getting closer. Cut to close up of great hairy legs pounding up the stairs of King Cool's castle. Cut back to the bedroom. The President suddenly notices some cloth and women's shawls lying in the corner of the room. He gives Hugh some of them.

PRESIDENT
Quick Hugh, ... cover yourself with these... I saw this in a movie once. Let me do the talking.

Cut to close up of the large hairy leg as it kicks open the door of the room. A tartan kilt swirls and a dagger hilt juts out from the top of a shabby white knitted knee sock. The door crashes open. Into the room storms an enormous and ugly monster of a man. This is the large Scottish giant mentioned in King Cool's note.

He is the eldest son of the giant who rules the kingdom of Scotland which is across the waters from Finn MacCool's kingdom in Ireland. The two kingdoms are linked by a great Causeway. The king of Scotland is known by everyone as Big Yin (The Big One) because of his enormous size, and his son is known as SOBY - Son of Big Yin. SOBY's appearance is rough and dishevelled. He is wearing the kilt and dress of a highland warrior. SOBY shouts in a crude, angry thunderous tone, with a thick Scottish accent.

SOBY
Where are they? Where's MacCool. Thinks he can protect them from the Big Yin.

CAMERA pans round as if from SOBY'S point of view. His eyes scan the room. He sees the outline of what looks like two old ladies, shawls cover their heads and shoulders. It is the President and Hugh in disguise - they are trembling. The President talks trying to shield his face from view.

PRESIDENT
(In a pronounced upper class English granny accent)
Can I help you sonny?

SOBY
(Shouts)
Who are you?

PRESIDENT
Oh, ah... I'm a... Maria Poppins at your service, baby-sitting service to the stars - and to kings of course - can I help you my good man?

SOBY
Where's MacCool? ...I want MacCool.

PRESIDENT
Are you a friend of his?

SOBY
Do I sound like I'm a friend... where is he? I've heard he's big, but he's no' as big as me. I'll tear him limb from limb.

PRESIDENT

So you've never actually met King Finn MacCool?

SOBY

No, we're not exactly your friendly neighbours next door you know ...quite the opposite.

PRESIDENT

And what do you want with King Finn MacCool?

SOBY

I wan'te kill him... along with those two other weirdos who are with him and have come from a strange land to visit him.

Hugh and the President look at each other and gulp.

SOBY

...Very weird they are I believe.

PRESIDENT

So what have they done these two... weirdos?

SOBY

It's not what they've done, it's what they could do ...if they're allowed to return to their world... it could ruin it for all of us. But don't you worry I'll soon find them... have you seen them at all?

HUGH

(Hugh tries to put on a Scottish accent)

Ach, hoots mon, oh no, no.

PRESIDENT

Oh no, we're just baby sitting here for King MacCool.

They point out to where the baby is lying in the cradle. The baby stretches out and growls threateningly.

SOBY

(He gulps)

Their baby! This is MacCool's b... b... baby?

He thinks to himself if this is MacCool's baby what sort of size is MacCool.

PRESIDENT

Oh yes... a bonnie wee lad isn't he? Takes after his father... who should be back at anytime now... Would you like to wait?

SOBY

...Oh... ah... no, not right now. Well I'm a goin'a have to get back for ma' tae. ... But you tell MacCool I'm looking for him, it's just I've got to go now... or I'll be late and I don't want to get into any trouble you know.

PRESIDENT

Oh right... can I say who called?

SOBY straightens himself up and proudly answers.

SOBY

Let me tell you this boy!... I am SOBY - I am, Son of Big Yin - the mighty and fearless leader of the Kingdom across the Great Causeway.

(Soby relaxes and winks at Baz and Hugh)

S-O-B-Y. Did you get that... son of Big Yin - clever isn't it... but my real name is actually Gerald... but everybody just calls me SOBY.

PRESIDENT

SOBY it is then.

SOBY

Here I can't stand gassin' here all day ... I better be 'aff.

SOBY exits through the door sheepishly then runs for his life, out of the castle and is seen to disappear over the distant hills.

PRESIDENT
(Still in a Mary Poppins accent)
Pity he couldn't stay - I was beginning to like that big man.

HUGH
Holy socks Baz that was a close one, come on let's get out of here before we're killed or something.

Suddenly King Cool who was dressed up as the baby rises up to his giant size from the baby's cradle. He takes a giant size baby's dummy out of his mouth.

KING COOL
What's the hurry?

The President and Hugh both scream out at the same time.

PRESIDENT
Ahaaaah ! ! !

HUGH
Ahaaaah ! ! !

King Cool takes off the baby hat from his head.

KING COOL
MacCool it you two - it's only me!

HUGH
My God Finn, you nearly frightened the life out of us just then. ...Do you know, I thought there was a real good family likeness with that baby.

PRESIDENT
Why you wily old fox, King Finn... let me tell you I'm mighty impressed...

KING COOL
We're a peace loving people in this land and that's the way I like to keep it. ...So if it means you have to use your brains rather than your sword arm to resolve a problem... then it's better for everyone.

PRESIDENT
Our world could learn a lot from you Finn.

KING COOL
And there's a lot more I must show you. Come I'll give you the tour.

They move outside of the castle to be welcomed by a happy, joyous cheering crowd.

EXT. KING COOL'S CASTLE - MORNING

1ST MAN
Well done King Finn MacCool.

1ST WOMAN
We love you King Finn.

King Cool, the President and Hugh all wave to the crowd and walk between them.

2ND MAN
You sure out-smarted that big, galoot SOBY.

PRESIDENT
...And he never even batted an eyelid.

2ND WOMAN
That's why he's our King Cool...

The sound of an up tempo, drum beat starts and the 'KING COOL' original theme song begins.

Members of the crowd partake in upbeat beautifully choreographed dance routines etc. King Cool walks in the middle between the President and Hugh, who are lifted shoulder high, like heroes, as they pass through the crowds. During the song the music level fades, the President congratulates King Cool on the genuine affection shown for him.

PRESIDENT
Now I know why you're the king around here... man, they just love you... and I know just the reason why.

KING COOL
Why's that?

PRESIDENT
Because you sure are... one cool MacCool...

They all laugh.

FADE TO BLACK.

The 'New' Democracy

7

The lush and enchanting sound of orchestral strings fade up and introduce through an intensely coloured dissolve, a wide-screen panorama of a most stunning and magical landscape. CAMERA pans over a countryside of happy smiling faces, with children playing and people enjoying life. CAMERA tracks towards a very grand public building surrounded by beautiful white marble columns. CAMERA zooms in towards the three figures of King Cool, the President and Hugh as they ascend the white marble steps leading up to the entrance of this most impressive building that looks somewhat similar to the Capitol Buildings in Washington D.C. Music fades.

EXT. STEPS OF THE ADMINISTRATION BUILDING - MID DAY

KING COOL

Does this look sort of familiar to you Mr. President? This is our administrative centre... where representatives of all the regions of our world, meet to plan and carry out the people's wishes.

PRESIDENT

You can't beat good old politics!

KING COOL

But not as you know it Baz - you see... we operate a system here that's different from yours. In ours, there's no corruption, no payoffs, no fund-raising, no primaries, no TV debates, no party politicing ...in fact, we have no Political Parties to divide us.

PRESIDENT

What? No Political Parties?... Come on Finn, without them... where's your democracy?

KING COOL

Democracy!! ... One day Baz, your people will learn that party politics only creates divisions among people and destroys democracy. ...Now you're going to find out how true democracy really operates.

PRESIDENT

The way it's always operated. ...Come on King Finn, you know human nature. It's impossible to have a system that can't be influenced by... you know - greed! Power! Ego! ...And money! ...Lots and lots of money... to name but a few.

KING COOL

There's nothing wrong with money Baz. It's the love of money and power... by self-serving people that is the problem. The important thing is to have a system that puts power in the hands of those people who can handle it. People who want to help everyone... not just themselves and their mates. ...Come on let me show you!

King Cool, the President and Hugh enter the impressive building. They walk down corridors, full of busy people and arrive into a main auditorium - a large gathering is assembled and in discussion.

INT. ADMINISTRATION BUILDING AUDITORIUM - MID DAY

KING COOL

(In hushed voice)

All these people are the elected representatives of cities, towns and villages throughout our land.

PRESIDENT

You see... good old politicians.

KING COOL

In our system Baz, these people don't decide to stand for election. They are chosen without them even knowing it.

PRESIDENT

How can you do that?

KING COOL
It's easy! Come let me introduce you here to Billy.

King Cool quietly puts his hand on the shoulder of the man sitting in front of him. He speaks to him in a hushed tone.

KING COOL
Billy, these are guests of ours - the President of America... and Mr. Hugh MacCool.

Billy turns around to speak to them.

BILLY
Welcome. Any friend of King Finn is specially welcome.

KING COOL
The President would like to know how you ended up representing your people here, without standing for election.

BILLY
Well it's the way we vote here. Once a year, across all our villages, towns and cities, we choose by secret ballot the individuals whom we believe will best serve the needs of all our people. When the votes are counted, the nine people with the most votes are asked to form a local administrative Council. Because we already know these people for their positive actions to serve all in our community... we are electing leaders with an already established, effective track record.

KING COOL
With your electoral system Mr. President... as you are well aware... to get elected... you make a lot of 'promises'...in order to convince people to vote for you. After you're elected...
(MORE)

KING COOL (cont'd)
delivering on those promises, becomes somewhat less important. And because your campaign needs lots of funding... you end up 'owing' many people. ...People whose vested interest may oppose the greater good of the general public. ...So you end up with a conflict of interest. ...And most important... to put yourself forward for election requires a certain type of personality and ego. People who tend to be smart talkers... lawyer types like yourself. Plus you need the right look... and are ambitious to seek positions of power. Our system... excludes no one... eliminates the corruptive influence of money... and people are chosen purely on their proven deeds... and ability to serve their community.

PRESIDENT
So Billy, you had no say in your election... at all?

BILLY
Nor would I want to - you see if you put yourself forward or canvas in any way to be elected - you're immediately eliminated from our election. This means everyone is free to vote for anyone, without feeling pressurized. And when I was selected as one of the nine, I had the option to decline my position. I believe however it was a great honour to be chosen by the people of my village... in a system that it is fair and where everyone has an equal chance to serve.

PRESIDENT
So in your system you only elect those who already have a tried and tested track record for genuinely helping people and have good leadership qualities.
(MORE)

PRESIDENT (cont'd)

Everybody knows who they are voting for - so you don't get any 'blow in' career politicians wanting to make a name for themselves. ...Plus you don't have all the wasted time and money for electioneering. That means important decisions in government are not delayed or fudged for fear of upsetting the voters at election time... and you also avoid the hypocritical party political speeches, the endless funding campaigns... and ridiculous fund-raising parties.

BILLY

Well... we still have lots of parties... but they're just... 'Fun-raising parties'.

They all try to suppress muffled laughter in order not to disturb the assembled gathering.

KING COOL

And then Billy was also elected to be the representative of his local area... at this our National Assembly - where the wider issues in the Community are discussed. Like this special meeting today... which has been called to deal with the surprise visit of our 'good friend' SOBY.

King Cool turns to the President and Hugh.

KING COOL

Your arrival in our world, could result in further action from his father... 'The Big Yin'. He lives in the land across the Great Causeway. Unfortunately as a race of people, they too, are yet to find the way to live in peace and harmony with one another. The Assembly is now consulting on what action we may have to take if Big Yin gets ugly.

CAMERA pans to a head table where the nine National Council members are seated. A female Council member addresses the meeting.

COUNCIL MEMBER 1
Assembled delegates... we welcome to our midst our beloved King Finn MacCool... who has with him two special guests. They visit us from another world and another time. ...However we meet today to discuss the visit of SOBY ...who has come in search of our special guests.

The Assembly acknowledge the President and Hugh. They wave politely in response.

COUNCIL MEMBER 1
We have seen how by the actions of our wise and astute King, that we have been able to buy some time. We know of old that SOBY's ruthless and cunning father Big Yin, will not be so easy to deter from a violent confrontation with our people. Delegates, we seek your advice and opinions on this matter.

A male Council member addresses King Cool.

COUNCIL MEMBER 2
Perhaps King Finn, you and your guests could come up to the podium to address our delegates with your thoughts.

King Cool, the President and Hugh acknowledge the request and move forward to sit down at the main platform. King Cool stands to address the Assembly.

KING COOL
Assembled delegates... before I speak, perhaps I would ask our guests to introduce themselves and tell us why they believe that they're here. Then perhaps we can all assess the best way to address this issue.

King Cool gestures to the President and Hugh to say something. The President pushes Hugh forward to speak.

HUGH

Who me?! Oh no Baz I'm a...

PRESIDENT

Go on... you're a natural, be yourself.

HUGH

(Hugh rather sheepishly and humbly addresses the Assembly.)

Well, ah, hello - I'm Hugh.

Five hundred plus assembled delegates answer in unison with a friendly but loud response.

DELEGATES

Hello Hugh!!

Hugh falls back in surprise and amazement at the volume of their response. Gingerly he pulls himself off the floor and speaks to the delegates.

HUGH

Th... th... thank you for your kind and welcoming... welcome. All I would like to say is that I haven't a clue where I am... or why I'm here... but I do know that you've all made me feel... as if I am at home.

Delegates laugh.

HUGH

In fact... you're all so very kind and nice... that... I actually feel more at home here than I do... when I am at home. So, good luck to you all.. and ... have a nice day!

Delegates applaud and cheer. The President steps forward to speak.

PRESIDENT

Thank you... thank you all... and Hugh, what a natural... God I wish I could have said that. However the sentiments of Hugh's words... were able to convey better than I can... just what our visit to your land has already taught me. I feel as if I'm in a dream. It's a dream however that is real... and in the short time I've been here, I've suddenly started to see... a new way to live... a new way to run an elected administration effectively... and a new way to behave collectively as people. It seems awfully simple - but then that's the hallmark of all the great ideas. However, I now also realize that it is very important for me to be able to return to my world... to share this new knowledge and experience, with the people in our world - believe me, the state that our world is in at present, we need all the help we can get... and... it can't come soon enough!

The President becomes very humble.

PRESIDENT

For this new insight and first hand experience... I must thank you all. You are very kind people... you are very wise and enlightened people. I have seen that you have somehow been able to park the whole human natures of ego, self and greed. These are vulnerable human traits that are at the core of the problems that we face in the world I live in. You have been able to replace the demands of serving self... by making your primary goal... service to others. By doing this, you can all live in peace and harmony... while enhancing your own individuality and self respect. I feel inspired... and while it would be easy to stay here with you... something inside me tells me that I must try to return...

(MORE)

PRESIDENT (cont'd)
and to somehow inform and educate the people in my world... to your system of real democracy. This is a system of governance that is truly run... for the people and by the people... and can prove for us to be... one giant leap for humankind !! God bless you all.

The assembled delegates smile and warmly applaud. King Cool steps forward.

KING COOL
And we must try to get you there... to fulfill your destiny.

The delegates positively indicate their approval.

KING COOL
I believe we must do whatever is necessary to protect our guests... even...

He pauses.

KING COOL
Even if we have to deploy... the Guardians of Justice.

Delegates gasp.

KING COOL
We recognize that the use of force is always our very last option. However, given the circumstances that we now face... if Big Yin tries to invade us... in order to kill our friends here... the assembled delegates must now make a collective decision... if it is time to fully mobilize 'The Guardians'.

All the delegates talk among themselves. Delegates vote on futuristic voting system with their hands placed on a screen in front of them. The result of the vote appears on a large screen above the platform. The result is positive. King Cool speaks to the Assembly.

KING COOL

Let it be so. I believe you have chosen wisely... let us make preparations.

Pic fades on close up of King Cool with the sound of delegates applause in the background.

FADE TO BLACK.

Flower Power

EXT. EDUCATION BUILDING - AFTERNOON

Pic fades up to show King Cool, the President and Hugh walking towards the entrance of another grand building

PRESIDENT
The Guardians of Justice! - who are they?

KING COOL
They are our 'Guardian Angels' - who help us to protect our people and maintain harmony... come on I'll show you.

King Cool leads the President and Hugh into the building, past a sign which says 'Education Centre'. They go into a class room location and see what looks like a bespectacled school teacher deeply engrossed with children in a discussion. The teacher acknowledges King Cool. He gestures for the teacher to continue his class. King Cool, the President and Hugh quietly chat to each other at the back of the room.

INT. CLASSROOM - AFTERNOON

KING COOL
This is Conor - a top ranked Commander in the Guardians.

The President and Hugh both look at Conor with surprise. Then they burst out laughing. All the children turn around to look at them.

PRESIDENT
This is the spearhead of your primary protection force? - Come on Finn - we're dead meat.

Hugh is seen to swallow hard.

KING COOL
Looks can sometimes deceive... You see there are two key elements to our protection system. One is education and spiritual detachment - the other is courage. Put them together and you have the qualities necessary to become a Guardian of Justice. Size isn't everything...
(MORE)

KING COOL (cont'd)
however, we do have a few bigger Guardians than Conor.

HUGH
I should hope so.

KING COOL
The Guardians are one of the vital elements who have enabled our world to live in peace and harmony. They are a practical example of the unity that exists throughout our world. The Guardians of Justice are a unified peace-keeping force made up from representatives of every region of our world. In our administration system we have set codes of conduct and standards for protecting the freedom of all citizens. Should any individual in any region be seen to use their own self interests or authority to break these codes by intimidation, threats or violence... the Guardians can act quickly and in unity to make these people answerable for their actions. It is amazing how rarely they require to be used. This is because everyone knows that there is no way that they can get away with abusing another citizen... without facing the consequences. This is real justice in action and it works.

PRESIDENT
Wow it's amazing - and it's so simple. Everyone acting for the common good. I'm afraid in our world at present real unity of purpose in protecting our Human Rights is lost in the endless divisions created by narrow minded, self interest in politics, nationalism, religion, and business. Our attempts to work together... such as The United Nations... usually ends up as a very costly talking shop for non-elected people with fairly ineffective results.
(MORE)

PRESIDENT (cont'd)
We simply don't have the unified system
or the political will to uphold real justice
throughout our world.

KING COOL
But with the right education, combined
with common sense, your world can
discover the source and identity of the
real enemy that divides people against
themselves and the common good. You
can expose the tactics it uses to create
and maintain disunity. If you treat people
the right way... with love and respect...
people can learn to change for the better.
...And right now it's time for you to meet
some 'very special people !!' ...
Come on!

King Cool gestures to the teacher to indicate their departure. The trio leave the classroom and move outside.

FADE TO BLACK.

EXT. COUNTRYSIDE - LATE AFTERNOON

Scene opens with King Cool, The President and Hugh walking through a magical and beautiful verdant country landscape with crystal clear rivers and flowers of every colour, glistening in the warm sunshine.

HUGH
Who are these 'special' people then?

KING COOL
The most important people in my kingdom.

PRESIDENT
Now they do sound important.

KING COOL
They are!

HUGH
Who are they then Finn? Are they like
really Big Giants?

KING COOL
Bigger

HUGH
God - they must be huge!

King Cool thinks he says Hugh.

KING COOL
How can they be you?

PRESIDENT
Finn, don't go there. Please, I couldn't take any more...

KING COOL
OK. We're going home to meet my beloved wife, the Queen, and our wonderful children - come on, help me pick some flowers for them.

HUGH
Pick flowers? Right! How will I know which ones to pick?

KING COOL
I think we might get some help!

Hugh bends down to pick a flower. Just before he does, a friendly face appears in the flower next to the one he was going to pick. The flower speaks to Hugh in a most polite and courteous tone.

FLOWER 1
Excuse me, but I really would feel most privileged and honoured if you would consider picking me.

Hugh responds without flinching at this most surreal event.

HUGH
God Baz, this place is so friendly, even the flowers speak to you!

The President sort of turns around having caught the end of Hugh's remark.

PRESIDENT
Indeed Hugh... the what speaks to you?

HUGH
The flowers! ... Look there's another one.

Hugh and the President look at a smiling face in a flower. Hugh speaks to it.

HUGH
Good afternoon Mr. Flower, how are you,
isn't it a fine day?...

The flower responds in a soft and friendly female voice.

FLOWER 2
It is indeed Mr. Hugh. It's a lovely day to
be picked.

The President looks on in disbelief. He is totally speechless. Another flower speaks.

FLOWER 3
Would you be picking your flowers for any
special occasion Mr. Hugh?

HUGH
Well sort of... you see we're going to King
Finn's home and he wants to give his wife
some flowers... I think he must like her a
lot.

Suddenly all around Hugh and the President, hundreds of beautiful flowers eagerly spring up out of the ground and start shouting out with wild excited but polite enthusiasm. A chorus of voices is heard from the flowers all requesting Hugh and the President to pick them.

FLOWERS
Pick me, pick me, please pick meeee...

PRESIDENT
I don't believe this, it's unreal.

HUGH
Isn't this great fun Baz - talking flowers.

PRESIDENT
I heard about some strange stuff in the days of 'flower power'... but this really is just too far out man... Hugh... just keep an eye out... I think there could be a few Umpa-lumpas around here?

The flowers continue with their request to be picked. A sunflower, stretches up to the level of the President's face and speaks to him in a deep but shy male voice.

FLOWER 4
Gosh Mr. President please pick me! It is the greatest honour us flowers can have, to be picked by King Finn himself as a love token for his beautiful Queen.

PRESIDENT
But you're all so beautiful... It's impossible to choose between you... I just can't decide.

FLOWERS
Oh pick me, pick me, pick me

HUGH
I've got it Baz... Right you flowers... what are you like at singing?

Suddenly the flowers all stop chattering in unison. One flower with a very shy and humble demeanor speaks up.

FLOWER 1
You want us to sing... you really want us to sing. ... Don't you know that's what flowers love to do best.

FLOWER 2
After looking pretty and smelling nice that is.

HUGH
That's brilliant sure, I love singing too...
OK, lets make it just like 'The Flower
Factor'... a sort of big karaoke for
flowers... and Mr. Baz and I will be judges.

The flowers all cheer in approval.

HUGH
Right now. Is there any particular song you
all want to sing?

FLOWER 2
Well, if you don't mind, we really love to
make it up as we go along.

HUGH
That's good for us... take it away in your
own time.

The flowers all arrange themselves like a choir and some of them form a flower orchestra which starts to play. The flowers begin to sing their song - 'Pick Me'. During the opening instrumental music, a group of bees swarm together to hum the intro chorus.

BEES
Buzz... buzz... buzz...
Buzz... buzz... buzz...

FLOWER 1
If you need to pick someone to thank your
love...

FLOWER 2
Or tell them they're the one you're always
thinking of...

CHORUS ALL FLOWERS
Then pick me... pick me... pick me... pick
me.

FLOWER 3
We'll perfume the air all around and
above.

FLOWER 4
To bring pleasure and joy to your one true love.

CHORUS ALL FLOWERS
So pick me... pick me... pick me... pick me.

FLOWER 5
We all come in different shapes

FLOWER 6
...and colors.

ALL FLOWERS TOGETHER
...But when you bunch us up together... we're all sisters and brothers.

CHORUS ALL FLOWERS
So pick me... pick me... pick me... pick me.

FLOWER 7
(Male, deep base)
But if you don't pick me now you needn't ask my pardon...

ALL FLOWERS TOGETHER
Because we all share... the same beautiful garden.

So pick him... pick her... pick him... pick her.

FLOWER 1
We're never no trouble...

FLOWER 4
...A perfect son...

FLOWER 3
...And daughter...

FLOWER 7
And all we ever ask is just a little bit a' water.

ALL FLOWERS TOGETHER
So... pick me... pick me... pick me...
pick me... pick me... pick me... pick me.

The buzzing bees join the flowers for a finale to the song as they fade into the distance.

During the song Hugh, the President and King Cool walk through a happy sea of singing and smiling flowers. They begin to pick flowers as they go, until they each have a beautiful large bouquet of stunning blooms. Song begins to fade... as our trio disappear from view into the distant, sun-filled, lush and verdant landscape.

FADE TO BLACK.

‘Cool’ New World

9

INT. KING COOL'S CASTLE - LATE AFTERNOON

Pic fades up on a close up of a beautiful large bunch of flowers. What we don't see is King Cool, the President and Hugh who are standing side by side to create a 'wall of flowers'. Suddenly a pair of female hands separates the flowers to reveal the warm and friendly face of King Cool's wife, Queen Suraya. She has a distinguished, gracious poise and moves with an air of calm serenity. She is elegantly dressed in a long flowing gown of white and gold, has long dark hair and the striking look of Asian royalty. She speaks in a polite and welcoming tone.

QUEEN SURAYA

These are for me? ... They are so beautiful. ... Thank you!

The Queen takes the bunch of flowers in her arms to reveal King Cool, the President and Hugh. King Cool leans forward, gives her a kiss and a warm embrace.

KING COOL

Nothing less would do for the most beautiful Queen in all the worlds.

QUEEN SURAYA

Come on Finn, you're embarrassing me in front of these gentlemen.

KING COOL

My apologies Suraya... what with being back late last night and our surprise visitor this morning... I didn't have the opportunity to introduce you to our special guests. These are the gentlemen I told you would be visiting us.

King Cool presents the President to the Queen.

KING COOL

This is the President of the United States of America... Mr. Abbas Obanna.

QUEEN SURAYA
I am most honoured to meet you Mr. President... you are most welcome to our home.

The President reaches out to politely shake hands with the Queen. He is very taken by the Queen's regal beauty, charm and grace.

PRESIDENT
The honour is entirely mine, Your Majesty... but look, everyone just calls me Baz.

QUEEN SURAYA
Oh, please call me Suraya.

King Cool introduces Hugh to the Queen.

KING COOL
And this is Mr. Hugh MacCool. A very loyal member of the MacCool family.

QUEEN SURAYA
It is always a pleasure to meet family members.

The Queen reaches over and kisses Hugh on the cheek. Hugh becomes very shy and embarrassed.

HUGH
Hello... I'm Hugh... but since my early childhood, family members have always called me...

(He pauses)

...Hugh.

QUEEN SURAYA
Well Hugh and Baz, make yourselves at home. Please don't hesitate to ask for anything you may require to make your stay with us a happy and enjoyable occasion.

The President turns on some of his politician's charm.

PRESIDENT
Now I can understand why these flowers were getting so excited and animated about being picked for you.

QUEEN SURAYA
Oh you've had that experience. ...The flowers here are great fun... I guess you're going to find a lot of new experiences here compared to your world.

PRESIDENT
So far, it's like a beautiful dream.

QUEEN SURAYA
Well it's time to experience some of our hospitality.

HUGH
Oh great... food... I'm famished, it must be the air here. Do you know I could eat a horse...

(He pauses)

As long as it doesn't start talking to me.

(He pauses again)

Dinner won't start talking to me... will it Suraya?

QUEEN SURAYA
No Hugh, I can guarantee you that dinner will not be talking to you. It is due to be served soon, so please join us in the Banqueting Hall when you are ready.

FADE TO BLACK.

INT. KING COOL'S CASTLE - EVENING

King Cool, the Queen and their charming young children, a boy and a girl, are seen relaxing after dinner with the President and Hugh in a beautiful sitting room in the castle. The children are happily playing on the floor with their toys.

PRESIDENT
You really have it all sorted Finn. I wish that the world where I come from, could experience all of this... and learn from your - 'Cool World'. So, what's the secret - how can we change our world.

KING COOL
You just said it.

PRESIDENT
I did?

HUGH
Ah now Baz you did right enough... whatever it was!

KING COOL
It's all about learning... At one time we behaved like your world. Where people jealously protect self-interest. This is what creates divided communities. What we eventually realized was that once you learn to overcome the demands of self - everyone benefits - especially yourself. It's Mankind's biggest mystery, but that's the simple answer... and it applies in all the worlds - even yours.

PRESIDENT
But we already have a very sophisticated learning system with schools and universities... how come we don't end up with happy balanced citizens - like you?

QUEEN SURAYA
Perhaps it's time for your educators to take a fresh look at the facts that people really need to learn, in order to produce fulfilled and happy people.

PRESIDENT
Yea, but what happens when some people, who are so deluded because they're conditioned by years of prejudice and hate that they don't want to learn... but only want to live by causing fear and terror? Like our fine family of psychos - the Big Yins.

KING COOL
Well at least the Big Yins are quite up front with their hatred and violence... So you know what you're up against.

QUEEN SURAYA
There are however many cunning and clever people who give the impression that they are serving the common good... Yet in truth, only seek to promote their own selfish aims - at any cost.

PRESIDENT
Yea... I've definitely met a lot of these people - trouble is, it's not always easy to spot them... till it's too late.

QUEEN SURAYA
That is why you must teach your people about the two natures we are all born with. Each nature comes with different motives and their actions produce different consequences. It's a key part of our growing up process as individuals to understand the outcomes that result from each of these natures. When we do - we really begin to mature our qualities as human-beings.

KING COOL

If the controlling demands of the self-nature are allowed to dominate - then the peace and harmony in our families and communities... will soon be destroyed. So if some people become so blinded by self... that they use violence and corruption to achieve their selfish aims... then as a last resort they must be confronted... with force.

QUEEN SURAYA

But remember you must act quickly and in unison to challenge these actions... otherwise cunning and devious minds can divide good people against themselves.

PRESIDENT

And to do that you have created an administration system that can respond efficiently, without being slowed down by bureaucracy, red tape or self-interest. Plus you have an election system that produces wise and caring leaders who only act for the common good.

HUGH

So how do you know, which one of the natures, wins out?

QUEEN SURAYA

That's a very good question Hugh... and I think was best summed up by some of the President's earliest citizens... the North American Indians.

PRESIDENT

They did? ... I think I'm about to learn something else.

QUEEN SURAYA

Yes indeed... their culture says that we are all born with two wolves inside us...

(MORE)

QUEEN SURAYA (cont'd)
A good wolf who cares for everyone in the community ...and a bad wolf ...whose evil motives mean they are only interested in themselves.

KING COOL
So, like Hugh... when a young Indian brave asked the question which wolf he would become...

QUEEN SURAYA
The wise Chief replied ...the wolf you become ...is the wolf you feed.

PRESIDENT
The wolf you feed! ...Wow ...that is so clever... Do you know, I think our country would be in better shape today ...if we'd listened to some of the wise counsel from our native American citizens.

QUEEN SURAYA
The world becomes a better place for everyone, when we can all learn to share our thoughts and counsel together, with respect and humility.

KING COOL
One day your people will learn that by sharing and caring for each other... rather than looking after self-interest... is the only way. You see in the big picture... we're all part of the same family.

CAMERA pans over the young children playing on the floor beside them.

QUEEN SURAYA
That's why all our children are brought up to understand this simple truth from the time they are babies.

PRESIDENT

You know, I didn't think this was possible. However, I have now seen it working in your world with great effect. I guess I'm learning by example.

HUGH

Learning, leadership and love... the three L's... sure that had to be the answer...

They all look at Hugh with bewilderment.

PRESIDENT

You have such a natural way of putting things Hugh, I don't know how you do it!

HUGH

Neither do I.

They all laugh. Then King Cool turns to the President.

KING COOL

But remember... it starts with having visionary leadership and having the type of electoral system that produces those leaders. ...As I said to you earlier to-day... our system excludes no one from becoming a leader... and you'll find that your world will become a much better and happier place when you have an electoral system that embraces the meek and the humble.

HUGH

Sure "the meek shall inherit the earth"... it's a prophecy of destiny!

PRESIDENT

Well with our electoral system and style of government at present... the meek don't get a look-in... our Political world is a real 'dog eat dog' jungle!

KING COOL
And look at the mess your jungle is in. That's why it's time to show them a better way.

PRESIDENT
But where do I start...? It means changing our whole political system.

KING COOL
Your Politicians will be among the last to seek change... so if you share this new vision directly with all the citizens of your world... you'll find that change will come a lot quicker.

HUGH
Politicians don't see the vision... they only feel the heat.

PRESIDENT
Hugh you're amazing!

KING COOL
And you're the leader chosen to teach your people Mr. President. ...That's why you're here. It's your destiny. One day your words and guidance will help to rebuild the Causeway between the hearts of all men and women in your world... and lead them to create a new system... that brings peace and harmony for everyone.

PRESIDENT
Wow! ... I'm afraid that sounds to me like some sort of unbelievable dream scenario... especially when you consider that... I'm only one guy and it would mean changing our whole administration structures of government. And before that... you have to get people to agree to it. ...You think I can do all that?

KING COOL
It's not going to change over night. The history of your world shows that change comes slowly.

PRESIDENT
As I said this morning ...the state our world is in at present ...change couldn't come quick enough!

KING COOL
Given the right timing and commonsense learning approach, your people could surprise you, just how quickly they could adapt to these new systems. It's just at present they've no idea that there's a better, less divisive and more effective way to be democratic. ...Unfortunately the new learning plan to bring about peace and harmony to your world has some-how got suppressed and buried... by those people whose gravy-train of greed and power depends on the old corrupt system remaining in place... while the vast majority of your citizens are left to suffer... in ignorance.

PRESIDENT
You mean, a Plan to create this new world... already exists in our old world?

KING COOL
Believe me, it's there... and when your people realize there's a new and better way for everyone to live... change will come a lot quicker than you imagine... and you're the man to help them find it!... Baz, I know you can do it!

HUGH
And by the way... you're not completely on your own - don't forget... there are two of us! ...Sure won't we make a great team?

The President turns to Hugh with a tear in his eye.

PRESIDENT
My good friend Hugh, I'm sorry how could I...?

The President gives Hugh a hug. Hugh looks sort of surprised and bemused but happily reciprocates the embrace in a real buddy way.

KING COOL
Believe me, you both can do it... however the difficult bit...

The President suddenly interrupts.

PRESIDENT
The difficult bit - you mean changing a world full of corruption, violence, division, greed, hypocrisy, poverty, ego and rampant self-interest... is the easy bit...!!

KING COOL
As I was about to say... if Big Yin has his way ...the difficult bit is going to be getting you back to your world in the first place.

HUGH
How do we get back then Finn?

KING COOL
The only way is back through the 'Golden Orb of Light and Time' submerged beneath the 19th Tower on the great Causeway - that was how you arrived here. ...It is the only link between our worlds. We understand that Big Yin is already amassing his army on the shores of his land at the opposite end of the Causeway. We believe he intends to take over the 19th Tower and then perhaps invade us to prevent your return.

HUGH
But I still don't get what we have done to get his sporran in such a twist.

KING COOL
Big Yin is simply acting under instructions. You see there are those who know the potential power of change that your new knowledge can bring about back in your world. So he has been ordered to stop you. It's the same old story - the bad guys stick together.

PRESIDENT
Yeah, but only for themselves.

KING COOL
Come on... it's time to get some rest. We may have a big day tomorrow... as we try to get you home!

FADE TO BLACK.

Tartan Terror

10

Fade up dramatic aggressive drum beating war music. Pic fades up to reveal a dark mist swirling over the encampment of Big Yin on the Scottish shoreline. CAMERA pans over thousands of Big Yin's Stormtroopers preparing for battle and zooms in towards the headquarters of Big Yin. Mix to inside the HQ. CAMERA tracks in on the large imposing and frightening figure of Big Yin as he calmly but cruelly tortures a prisoner on a medieval human stretching rack. Beside him is SOBY. While smaller in stature than SOBY, Big Yin has a much more mean and cruel demeanor. He is attired in the tartan battle-dress of a highland warrior King and his presence strikes fear into all of those around him.

INT. BIG YIN'S SHORELINE ENCAMPMENT - NIGHT

BIG YIN

Our orders to destroy these intruders from
that other world... gives me the chance
I've been waiting for - to conquer the
lands of that smart arse Finn MacCool.

Big Yin calmly moves the torture rack up a notch. The prisoner screams out in pain.

SOBY

Aye - a big smart arse that's all he is.

Big Yin moves the rack another notch. The prisoner screams out again.

BIG YIN

Unfortunately he's too smart for you, you
big eejit - falling for that baby disguise...
how could ye be such a big Jesse?

Big Yin shakes his head and turns to walk away in disgust. As he does, he hits a lever to release the prisoner from the rack. The prisoner collapses to the floor writhing in pain. SOBY follows after Big Yin.

SOBY

I'm really sorry daddy... but don't ye
worry... I'm goin' te make it up to ye!

Big Yin stops and turns to SOBY.

BIG YIN

And how are ye goin' te do that?

SOBY
Well... I thought that I would kill him!

BIG YIN
That would be a start.

SOBY
Oh yes, I'll have him, don't you worry. Let me tell you this Da... if he thinks he can pull another fast one on me... he's got it coming to him this time... oh yes. Nay bather... when I get...

Big Yin rudely interrupts, grabs SOBY by the arm and starts to hustle him outside.

BIG YIN
When you get a move on - no more talk... come on... we've got a few surprises lined up for this big smart arse. ...It's time to put an end to... King Finn MacCool !!

FADE TO BLACK.

Mix to scene outside the Big Yin encampment. As CAMERA pulls out from Big Yin's HQ we see thousands of troops assembled, beginning to march in formation towards the Great Causeway.

FADE TO BLACK.

INT. BEDROOM OF FINN'S CASTLE - MORNING

Pic fades up to show the President and Hugh asleep in their beds. Early bird-song can be heard as the dawn sunlight begins to fill the room. Into the tranquil setting, King Cool is quietly seen to arrive. He gently wakens them.

KING COOL
Come on you two - we'll have to get a move on.

Hugh and the President begin to wake up, rub their eyes and yawn.

HUGH
Oh God Finn! Thank goodness you woke me up... I thought I was about to be eaten by a huge squidgy marshmallow.

KING COOL
You should be so lucky.

PRESIDENT
What is it Finn?

KING COOL
Big Yin's army is on the move towards the Great Causeway - come on - we've got to get ready quickly!

FADE TO BLACK.

Pic fades up to show the Council Chambers in the Administrative Centre. Members of the National Council are assembled with the leaders of the Guardians of Justice who are now attired in their stunning white and gold battle suits. King Cool, the President and Hugh enter the room.

INT. COUNCIL CHAMBERS - MORNING

KING COOL
Mr. President, Hugh... you know everyone here including this gentleman...

King Cool turns to an impressive and immaculately turned out Guardian in resplendent battle uniform.

KING COOL
This is Conor - you met him yesterday in class with the children.

Hugh and the President pause for a double take.

PRESIDENT
Excuse me... this... is Conor!
Wow - you guys sure do dress up well.

HUGH
God Baz I'm frightened of him... and he's
on our side!!

The Leader of the Council, a gently spoken lady, calls the meeting to order.

COUNCIL LEADER
King Finn, honoured guests and fellow
Councillors... please let us sit down... we
have little time. Big Yin's army is already
advancing towards the Great Causeway.

They all sit down around a large table. They look at a map and drawings spread out on the table

COUNCIL LEADER
We believe that Big Yin plans to march
onto the Causeway and take control of the
19th Tower where the 'Golden Orb of Light
and Time' is located.

COUNCIL MEMBER
Then what?

KING COOL
My guess is that he'll use this opportunity
to come after me and take over our
kingdom - he's been wanting that for a
long time. But perhaps this is our
opportunity to rid ourselves from Big Yin's
threats and bullying once and for all.

CONOR
How can we do that King Finn?

KING COOL
The Guardians are the finest trained and
equipped protection force known in our
worlds. Big Yin's army does, however,
outnumber them 200 to 1. Those are
significant odds.

HUGH
Those are suicide odds Finn. ...Are you serious? 200 to 1... these guys might be good but come on... give them a break !

Council Members murmur with disquiet at the startling imbalance of the odds. Suddenly King Cool looks up with excitement.

KING COOL
That's it! ... Hugh's right... he is a genius - what a great idea!

HUGH
(Looking stupefied)
It was?

PRESIDENT
(Looking just as bemused)
It was?

KING COOL
Look here...

They all look at the maps. King Cool points towards the drawings of the Great Causeway. CAMERA zooms in to see drawing detail.

KING COOL
The Great Causeway is the only link between us and Big Yin. There's only one way in... and there's only one way out.

PRESIDENT
Excuse me Finn, why can't you just go by ship across these waters, why do you need the Causeway in the first place?

Council Members all look at each other.

KING COOL
These are no ordinary oceans... unfortunately they are the legacy of previous generations - your generations Mr. President...
(MORE)

KING COOL (cont'd)
they have left them so polluted with toxic and radio active waste that no buoyant materials can survive its corrosive power... only the granite and basalt rock that the Great Causeway is made from... can withstand these destructive waters.

COUNCIL MEMBER
And if man or beast falls into this polluted soup, death is nigh on instant.

HUGH
Oh, great!

COUNCIL LEADER
That's why the Golden Orb at the 19th Tower is the vital key to all our plans - the water around its narrow confines provides the only pure and uncontaminated escape portal that enables us to travel from this world...

The Council leader looks at the President and Hugh.

COUNCIL LEADER
And ...it's the only way back to your world...

KING COOL
And that's why Hugh's idea might work.

Hugh and the President look at each other.

KING COOL
Big Yin and his army have stolen a march on us. ...His advance party of troops will have taken over the 19th Tower before any of our Guardians can get there. In conventional conflicts we may hope to out-flank his army from here and here.

He points to the maps.

KING COOL

Because we are confined to travel only on the Causeway, we have to meet the enemy head on... I don't believe with the size of Big Yins forces we could ever battle through to the 19th Tower... What's more, if we fail in our efforts, he could wipe out our entire battalions of Guardians... leaving the Causeway clear for his army to have an undefended route into our kingdom. His thugs would be free to ransack and pillage our land... destroying our homes... and killing our families!...

A worried and fearful look falls on all assembled.

KING COOL

So when Big Yin's advance troops take the 19th Tower... we must somehow... create a break... in the Great Causeway - a buffer that will isolate them from the main body of his army, before they arrive.

COUNCIL LEADER

A break in the Causeway ...that's easier said than done - especially with Big Yin's advance troops already protecting the area around the 19th Tower.

HUGH

Yeah, its not like they're going to step aside and say... oh! Right! Certainly, go ahead - blow up the Causeway!

KING COOL

That's why we've got to find a way past their advance forces without them seeing us.

COUNCIL LEADER

But the sides of the Causeway have a sheer drop into the polluted oceans.

KING COOL
We must think of a way.

COUNCIL LEADER
You'll have to think quickly.

KING COOL
(Takes on a sombre tone in his voice)
We must also prepare to create another break in the Causeway - my friends.

CONOR
Why's that King Finn?

KING COOL
To protect our homeland. When all the Guardians have made it onto the great Causeway approximately one mile offshore - we must detail a team of engineers to remain there. If we are not successful in our quest to overcome Big Yin's forces and he breaks through our lines, then we must destroy the Causeway at this point to stop his troops reaching our land.

He points to the map.

KING COOL
However, it will be obvious to you that by taking this action... we will cut off our one and only means of escape. ... For all Guardians... they will virtually be signing their own death warrant!

CONOR
That is why we are Guardians! If it means our world and our families will escape from the destruction of Big Yin's army. Then it is a small price to pay - we have pledged to give protection and service to all our people - whatever the cost.

PRESIDENT

Such courage and service to your people, is worthy of great honor. You have shown me once more by your example, the selfless commitment and inner strength needed to face any challenge.

CONOR

Mr. President... our true fulfilment comes from being able to face the enemies of freedom as a spiritual warrior. ...In that capacity, our service is timeless and immortal across all the worlds - that is why we have no fear of facing death in this or any world.

COUNCIL LEADER

Then let it be so. If necessary the Great Causeway will be destroyed behind you and your people will honor forever the name of the Guardians of Justice as immortals in this world.

KING COOL

Come! We must proceed immediately to the Great Causeway. Let us hope for some divine inspiration along the way to help us find a solution to Big Yin's challenge to our freedom.

FADE TO BLACK.

Picture fades up to show rows of battle-clad Guardians marching in perfect symmetry. King Cool is at the front in a stunning gold chariot drawn by four splendid white horses. Hugh and the President stand either side of him in the chariot.

As they travel past King Cool's castle his family are waiting outside. Music mood is sad and tearful. King Cool stops the chariot and dismounts. He first of all embraces his children and then says a sad farewell to his Queen.

EXT. IN FRONT OF KING COOL'S CASTLE - AFTERNOON

KING COOL
(Whispers in the Queen's ear)
Oh Suraya ...you are my today, my tomorrow, my eternity.

The Queen remains dignified, but with tears in her eyes.

QUEEN SURAYA
Oh Finn.

They embrace.

KING COOL
Take care of these little ones while I'm away - come on it's going to take more than a few bully boys to keep me from my family.

QUEEN SURAYA
Take this Finn.

She gives him a circular pendant made of gold from her neck.

QUEEN SURAYA
It carries within it all my love. ...Let it protect you from the blows of treachery and injustice. Keep it close to you... till we are once again reunited.

KING COOL
Should this day expose our physical frailties... remember that the invisible bond of our souls can never be parted. For all eternity we are as one.

They embrace and kiss again. Tearful music reaches a dramatic finale as they say their farewells. King Cool, the President and Hugh wave good-bye to the Queen and then set off towards the Great Causeway.

FADE TO BLACK.

The Straight and Narrow

11

Pic fades up on King Cool followed by his army of Guardians, as they emerge from a pass in the mountains. A wonderful panorama of the ocean is revealed before them. Then suddenly - stretching majestically out into the sea and far into the distant horizon, the spectacular architectural structure of the Great Causeway comes into view. Its outline glistens like gold in the late afternoon sun. Majestic twin towers formed out of the columns of the hexagonal shaped rock make a stunning grand entrance to the Causeway. Far in the distant horizon we see the dramatic outline of the nineteenth tower located right at the centre point of the Causeway. Its imposing outline reaches up like some futuristic city skyscraper high up into the sky. Music builds to an epic crescendo reflecting the scale of this spectacular scene. King Cool leads the Guardians onto the Causeway. Crowds wave and cheer them, throwing flowers as they pass. King Cool talks to Hugh and the President as they begin to travel out along the massive structure of the Great Causeway.

EXT. THE ENTRANCE TO THE GREAT CAUSEWAY - AFTERNOON

HUGH
Wow!

PRESIDENT
Impressive engineering Finn.

HUGH
It's a wonder.

PRESIDENT
They say it's one of the seven wonders of the ancient world.

KING COOL
Hey, not so much of the ancient if you don't mind!

They start to travel along the Great Causeway.

KING COOL
You know, when I'm on the Great Causeway, it always reminds me of the simple rules for living and finding true happiness.

HUGH
I think I'm about to learn something.

PRESIDENT
Can we tape this for posterity Finn...
sorry... just kidding.

King Cool strikes an imperious regal pose.

KING COOL
The Great Causeway... is like the road we
all must travel to live the perfect life
...very straight and very narrow.

King Cool looks out over the Causeway.

KING COOL
On either side of that road are the great
oceans of human desolation. Should we
deviate from that narrow path... we slide
into the great depths of self destruction
and death.

Hugh and the President both gulp. King Cool points to the ocean on their right side.

KING COOL
This ocean on the right represents the self-
destruction of the material world. The love
of wealth, position and power... just like
these glistening waters... they look
enticing, but hide within their depths... a
prison of unfulfillment and endless sorrow.

He then points to the ocean on their left side.

KING COOL
This ocean on the left, represents to me,
the destruction of self in the spirit. Those
people who immerse themselves in the
pious hypocrisy of their own
righteousness. They deceive themselves
and others that only their belief is the
right one.
(MORE)

KING COOL (cont'd)
They heed not the guidance of their Great Creator... Instead, in the name of their God... they make up their own words and interpretations to embellish their self-driven egos. They shut their minds to the truth... they become prejudiced in their attitudes and behavior. Their delusion is a cause and source of confusion and division among all of humanity. ... You see, it's only by keeping an honest and balanced perspective that you can keep your feet on the straight path. As with this Great Causeway... it's only when you fix your gaze, straight ahead towards the 'Golden Orb of Great Light'... that we can achieve the harmony and inner peace... that all humankind desires.

King Cool looks towards the 19th Tower of the Great Causeway and again his gaze seems to freeze in the epic pose of a great Biblical leader. Music swells as the CAMERA sweeps up over the Causeway towards the 19th Tower, where the outline of Big Yin's troops come into focus. They have taken up position in front of the 19th Tower to stop the advance of King Cool. The skies begin to darken as storm clouds appear on the horizon. Thunder and lighting approaches from a distance. Hugh's voice starts to tremble as he sees the massed ranks of Big Yin's warriors.

HUGH
An...an... and sometimes... even on the straight and narrow... you'll find some big eejit and his army... ready to smash your head in!!

KING COOL
That, my friend... that's when we must summon our inner courage ...and confront head-on, those who want to destroy our peace and stop our progress.

PRESIDENT
(Looking at the scale of Big Yin's warriors advancing towards them)
(MORE)

PRESIDENT (cont'd)

Look here Finn, I don't want to be rushing you... but, have you been able to work out yet, how we might separate Big Yin's advance troops from his main army.

KING COOL
Not yet Baz, though I was sort of hoping for some divine inspiration just there during my rather over-the-top sermon on the secrets of life and happiness... but I'm afraid... I got nothing!

PRESIDENT
Can I make a suggestion?

KING COOL
By all means.

PRESIDENT
I take it in your world we can't just fly over and bomb the living daylights out of them. ...We tend to do that a lot in our world.

KING COOL
No Mr. President, that's an option that's been eliminated in our world. ...Look where it's got you in your world.

PRESIDENT
And the oceans are instant death for anyone who goes near them.

KING COOL
Right.

HUGH
Oh God, we're totally...

The President interrupts.

PRESIDENT
Now, now, Hugh, it's time for a streak of inspiration.

HUGH

A streak of lightning more like!

They all go quiet and look pensive. Searching for ideas... suddenly lightning flashes over-head followed by a loud crack of thunder. The President quickly pulls on the reigns of the chariot and the horses come to a stop.

PRESIDENT

That's it... Hugh, you are a genius!

The President kisses Hugh on the forehead.

HUGH

OK, that's it, sure I knew that would be the solution... now what is it Baz - or have you just flipped?

PRESIDENT

Listen, you know we sort of travelled back in time in order to travel forward so we could arrive here in the future...

Hugh looks bemused.

PRESIDENT

Well, you remember what happened in the film 'Back to the Future' ...with the professor?

HUGH

God, I love that film Baz... you know every time I would fire up the 'Silver Streak'... I imagined I was in that Delorean! Do you know it was made just down the road from where I live.

KING COOL

What was?

PRESIDENT

The Delorean!

HUGH

The Delorean!

KING COOL
Oh right! How can the 'Delorean' - whatever it is, help us?

PRESIDENT
Well, if the professor was able to attract the lightning to fire up the Delorean... so can we!

HUGH
That's great... but just one thing, Baz... where are you going to get a Delorean out here in the middle of the ocean? And even if you did, how are we going to get it past a few thousand of Big Yin's troops without them seeing it...

PRESIDENT
(Looking thoughtful and pensive)
We won't need a Delorean car Hugh... we just need to create a few lightning bolts of our own... to sort out all of these big thugs.

KING COOL
Well now Mr. President, I believe your idea, might just work. They say lightning doesn't strike in the same place twice... well we might just have to do something to change that. Come on, I think this would be a very good time to open up negotiations with Big Yin.

Pic starts to fade as we see King Cool, the President and Hugh huddle together in conversation. Thunder and lightning flash across a dramatic sky... as a rousing fanfare of music heralds the imminent conflict.

FADE TO BLACK.

EXT. THE 19TH TOWER ON GREAT CAUSEWAY - EVENING

Scene opens with dramatic shot of Big Yin and SOBY standing astride the Great Causeway, in front of hundreds of his storm troopers. Behind them is the dramatic and imposing outline of the 19th Tower. King Cool, the President and Hugh arrive on their chariot and stop directly in front of Big Yin and SOBY. Big Yin speaks in a thunderous and threatening Scottish accent.

BIG YIN
And where do you think you're 'aff to MacCool?

KING COOL
And what authority gives you the right to block my way over the Great Causeway?

Big Yin replies in a condescending, put-down manner.

BIG YIN
My authority and my right - you snivelling yellow-bellied coward of a so-called leader - who has to dress up as a baby rather than fight like a man. ...You're only a Big Jesse.

KING COOL
Your right to what?

BIG YIN
My right to stop those two weirdo foreigners beside you... from returning to their world through the 'Orb of Light' in the 19th Tower.

SOBY steps forward and interrupts.

SOBY
Do you want me to kill them now, fearless leader?

Big Yin puts his arm out to hold back the advancing SOBY.

BIG YIN

Come on MacCool, hand them over, and I'll spare your humiliation and the elimination of your BG BG's.

KING COOL

Excuse me Big Yin you've lost me there - BG BG's ???

BIG YIN

Big girls' blouses of so called Guardians.

The Guardians react in a defiant tone.

KING COOL

For your own health's sake Big Yin, you really don't want to get on the wrong side of the Guardians ... but here, let me think about your offer.

The President, Hugh and the Guardians all groan with discernment and surprise at Finn's response to even consider Big Yin's offer to hand over the President and Hugh.

KING COOL

You say you'll spare us if we give you the two foreigners.

BIG YIN

You have my word.

KING COOL

(Under his breath)

I should be so lucky.

King Cool then speaks to Big Yin.

KING COOL

Big Yin, let us have a trial... prove to me that these men are not worthy to return to their world... and you can have them...

King Cool's troops gasp in disbelief. The President and Hugh are shell-shocked at their betrayal by King Cool.

KING COOL

And in return I will spare your wannabe Bravehearts from total annihilation by the Guardians of Justice. As you well know... the Guardians have eradicated the armies of every upstart dictator in this world... They'll be happy to add your tartan thugs to that list.

Big Yin's troops mutter with concern at this thought - because they are fearful of the Guardians' renown and legendary reputation.

BIG YIN

(In an aside to his troops)

Shut-up! You load of spineless rats.

He then speaks to King Cool.

BIG YIN

Very well then MacCool - a trial it is - but none of your fancy tricks or I'll see to it that after we destroy your Guardian Jesses,... I will personally supervise the elimination of every woman and child in your kingdom.

KING COOL

(In an aside to Hugh and the President who still look stunned at what's happening before them.)

Unfortunately I believe he means it - but still, - I think it's worth the risk.

King Cool addresses everyone on the Causeway.

KING COOL

A trial it is then... But look at the gathering storm clouds... and darkness is already setting in... let the trial take place at first light in the morning.

Lightning flashes and thunder cracks overhead. Big Yin looks to the sky.

BIG YIN

I'll agree to this adjournment on one condition MacCool... we put the alien scum under guard till the trial in the morning. Let us both pick twelve guards each to jointly watch them. So there's no chance of your tricks MacCool... I want these weirdos in full view all the time. To make sure of that... I've a little plan of my own.

KING COOL

You bargain hard Big Yin - but let it be so.

Hugh and the President are taken hold of by the Guardians. Before they are taken off they speak to King Cool. The President is aggressive and agitated - he starts to shout abuse at King Cool. Guardians restrain him.

PRESIDENT

Call yourself a king, MacCool? You're nothing but a low-down hypocrite who breaks his promises... you gave us your word, but typical, when the chips are down, you're nothing but a self-protecting coward.

At this remark King Cool steps forward and he is seen to strike the President with a mighty blow across the face. As he strikes out lightning flashes and thunder is heard.

KING COOL

(Aggressively)

I am the king around here and I make the decisions about what is right and wrong... Take them away!!

More lightning and thunder. King Cool turns away in anger, the President falls to the ground. He is surrounded by the Guardians. Big Yin condescendingly looks on and a cruel smirk rolls across his face. The Guardians pick up the President who is unconscious and drag him towards a raised parapet on the edge of the Causeway. Hugh shouts back at King Cool as he is being led away.

HUGH

You're going to regret this King Finn MacCool... I thought we were friends - but you'll pay for this...

He points to the motionless President.

HUGH

He's from America you know and they don't take too well to mistreating their own. I wouldn't like to be in your shoes when they hear about this!!

Thunder cracks across the sky.

HUGH

Listen to that!! Even God will take his vengeance on you.

King Cool gets back onto his chariot and speaks to himself.

KING COOL

Let's hope so!!

The President and Hugh are tied to the sloped parapet on the side of the Causeway which drops directly into the poisonous seas below. A single rope is tied to a stone on the Causeway which is stopping the President and Hugh from falling into the sea. Big Yin walks towards the rope and draws his large sword.

BIG YIN

Any trickery from anyone before the trial...

He wields his sword towards the rope and stops half an inch before cutting it.

BIG YIN

And we won't need a trial.

(He sniggers scornfully)

SOBY reaches forward, pulls out his sword and threateningly raises it over his head.

SOBY
Look Da ...why don't I just make those two 'deed' right now... and we can all go home for our tae.

Big Yin holds back SOBY.

BIG YIN
No, not yet. I think I'm going to enjoy our little court-room drama with MacCool here!... But just to be on the safe side, I think I should take out a little insurance policy.

KING COOL
What do you mean?

BIG YIN
I mean that if these two don't quite make it to the trial... maybe their death may not mean that much to you after all... So I'm going to take a little precaution and add a second condition to our deal.

KING COOL
A second condition - no way - a deal is a deal.

BIG YIN
Then the deal is 'aff MacCool - sure we can go ahead and kill them here and now!...

SOBY raises his sword again.

SOBY
Just say the word Da and I'll finish them now!

Big Yin's soldiers move threateningly towards the President and Hugh. King Cool's Guardians move quickly in to protect both of them.

BIG YIN
I see we have a bit of a stand-off MacCool.

KING COOL
What's your second condition?

BIG YIN
Well, if perhaps you have no loyalty to these two wimps, perhaps you'll not keep your end of the deal. That's why you must give me someone for whom I know you feel much loyalty and affection... to be included in our little nest of hostages... oh sorry... I mean guests.

KING COOL
And who do you have in mind?

BIG YIN
Why... your very own Queen of hearts of course ...Mrs. Finn MacCool... ha, ha,ha!

Big Yin laughs sarcastically. King Cool gets very angry and agitated. He is dumbstruck and paralysed by such a request. He falls to the floor of his chariot - he was not expecting this. He holds his head in his hands trying not to let his troops see the anguish of his dilemma. Big Yin's voice is heard to boom out.

BIG YIN
What is it - oh mighty and fearless leader... cat got your tongue?

(He again laughs sarcastically)

Surely you're not going to let a little thing such as a woman bring the mighty giant MacCool to his knees... Why you are a pathetic insult to the male species.

As Big Yin is hurling his insults, CAMERA cuts to a close up of King Cool crouched down in his chariot. King Cool mutters in anguish to himself.

KING COOL
What am I to do? What am I to do? Please Suraya - what must I do?

Suddenly we see a small translucent hologram mirage of Queen Suraya reflecting on the golden surface of King Cool's chariot. Queen Suraya speaks in a calm and dignified tone.

QUEEN SURAYA

You must do, and I must do, what our honoured positions as King and Queen demand. We must detach ourselves from all personal feelings and emotions to follow only the path of justice and truth for the benefit of all the worlds - and not just to consider our personal desires to be together. Don't you know... our love is eternal, it will never end... regardless of what is to happen to us now or in the future. I'll have them prepare my fastest stallion... I'll be there with much haste - remember my King, every such test makes us stronger warriors in the spirit of love.

Queen Suraya's image fades. King Cool is seen to rise from behind his chariot. Big Yin speaks out.

BIG YIN

Did my little extra condition pose you some problems, King Finn MacCool?

KING COOL

Not in the slightest - you big oaf of a Haggis - I was just having some problems with my personal mobile communicator here...

(He looks down inside the chariot)

But it's OK now. Queen Suraya will arrive in two hours.

Big Yin speaks to SOBY beside him.

BIG YIN

Personal mobile communicator? ...Loaf of a Haggis? What gibberish is he talking about now?

SOBY

Ye see... no matter how big they are... they all crack sometime or other. Put them under pressure and kersplat!... They're right off their heed!

KING COOL

But I too have one condition that you must honour! ... You spare our Queen the trauma and indignity of hanging up there overnight with the other two... and you personally look after her in your own headquarters.

Big Yin looks pleasantly surprised by this condition of King Cool.

BIG YIN

That's not a condition MacCool... That would be a pleasure...

KING COOL

But I warn you, lay one finger on her and I'll hunt you down like the dog you are. And when I find you... you'll wish that death had taken you long before that day... as the vengeance I seek... will be greater than all the fires of hell.

BIG YIN

Good show MacCool - that's more like it... I do love to stir the animal beast within you... makes it more of a sporting challenge don't you think?

Conor the Guardian commander runs over to King Cool's chariot.

CONOR

King Finn you can't do this, the Queen must be protected... you said it yourself.

King Cool whispers to Conor.

KING COOL
Sometimes Kings and Queens must act with the responsibility their station gives them. Conor... this is such an occasion. The Queen will actually arrive within the hour. Set up my temporary headquarters at Tower 18 South. I've bought some time to prepare the Queen, before taking her to Big Yin in the 19th Tower.

King Cool then shouts over to Big Yin.

KING COOL
My Guardian Commanders will inspect your sadistic little toys to see that they meet the convention on prisoners' rights.

BIG YIN
Convention on prisoners' rights - what the blazes is he on about?

SOBY
I told ye Da ... he's right off his heed.

BIG YIN
And when can we expect Queenie?

KING COOL
I'll bring her to you when she arrives.

Each side nominates a dozen troops to form a guard. The President still lies unconscious. Hugh can be heard fearfully protesting his innocence and tries to stir the President.

HUGH
Come on Baz, wake up, you've got to do something.

The President however remains motionless.

FADE TO BLACK.

Back to the Future

12

Big Yin and SOBY return to their headquarters located in the 19th Tower. The interior is impressively futuristic in style. They enter one of the splendid upper rooms.

INT. ROOM IN 19TH TOWER - EVENING

SOBY

Man dear, that was smart, Da... the way that you out manoeuvered MacCool on that hostage deal.

BIG YIN

Never underestimate MacCool. Beneath that goody-two-shoes facade lies a very intelligent and perceptive brain... However I do think it was a bit of a master stroke to get mother MacCool as our hostage. She's the one person who guarantees that he won't risk trying any of his tricks. Frankly I didn't think he would go for it!!... So you're right... sometimes I just amaze myself how smart I am... because the Big Yin always rises to the challenge. And that's why I'm the King... So, son of Big Yin... I hope you're learnin' somethin' here, 'cause up to now... you've been very, very, disappointin'...

SOBY

Don't you worry Da, I've been takin' it all in... One day I'll make you proud, when I'm a big smart arse like yourself!

Big Yin looks at SOBY with surprise.

SOBY

Oh, no... I mean... ah like I don't mean... that you are a smart arse... what I mean is that you're real smart and clever like... you know.

BIG YIN
(Sighs in despair)
Why do I bather?...

FADE TO BLACK.

EXT. QUEEN ARRIVES ON THE GREAT CAUSEWAY - EVENING

CAMERA pans over the dramatic expanse of the Great Causeway at dusk. Melancholy tones of serene Irish ballad music fade up along with the sound of a horse galloping. CAMERA zooms in on Queen Suraya as she rides alone at pace on her white steed along the Great Causeway. Eventually she begins to slow and rides through the ranks of the Guardians of Justice. She arrives at King Cool's overnight headquarters, set up in Tower 18 South. The Queen is escorted by a Guardian to a room where King Cool is waiting for her. Queen Suraya and King Cool meet in a passionate and loving embrace.

INT. KING COOL'S HEADQUARTERS 18TH TOWER - EVENING

KING COOL
Oh Suraya, I'm so sorry you had to be involved with this.

QUEEN SURAYA
I feel so much better now that I'm here with you... and anyway it could be exciting!

KING COOL
But Big Yin is so unpredictable, he's capable of anything... are you sure you want to go through with this?

QUEEN SURAYA
No, I'm not... but under the circumstances ...what alternatives do we have?

KING COOL
Ah!... None!

QUEEN SURAYA

Well... let's get on with it... You never know, it may prove valuable to have someone close to Big Yin at this time. If I find out anything I'll try to get a message to you.

KING COOL

To-night, if you can try to keep Big Yin occupied... we're planning a little surprise for him and his thugs around midnight. So don't be alarmed if you start to hear some loud bangs. It's just part of our plan to separate Big Yin's advance troops - at this moment based around the 19th Tower, from the massed ranks of his main army on the shore. They are due to begin advancing at dawn onto the Great Causeway... Anyway that's the plan, whether it works or not... is the big unknown.

QUEEN SURAYA

Still it's worth the risk, you have to do something before morning... and you did well to stall for time. ...Let's try to use it to good effect.

KING COOL

And this has only been made possible because of you. Your courage had bought us time... you are a true Queen to our people. I didn't think it was possible to love you more than I already do... but now... in the face of death, my love for you has soared to a new dimension.

Tears fill the Queen's eyes, and they hold each other in a loving embrace.

QUEEN SURAYA

You are my inspiration Finn. I've learnt from your selfless devotion in the face of the enemy... You have taught me well, and it is now time for me to fulfill my duty as your Queen... I love you Finn.

They warmly embrace once again. A tear rolls down King Cool's face. Music swells in a tender heartbreaking scene. King Cool and the Queen leave his Headquarters. They mount his chariot, and begin to head towards the 19th Tower. As they approach the tower, they look up to the parapet where the President and Hugh are suspended. They slowly proceed past the warrior Stormtroopers of Big Yin. They arrive at the 19th Tower where they are met by Big Yin and SOBY.

EXT. THE 19TH TOWER - EVENING

KING COOL

I have honoured my end of the deal Big Yin... make sure you keep yours by showing Queen Suraya the respect that her position commands.

BIG YIN

(Turns to Queen)

Your presence honours us your Majesty... I know that I'll feel much safer with you close to me at this time.

Big Yin turns to King Cool.

BIG YIN

However one wrong move by you MacCool and you can say goodbye to this pretty face.

Big Yin threateningly runs his finger nail down the side of the Queen's face. She thwarts off his advances with disdain.

BIG YIN

Oh! She's a fiery one MacCool... beneath that cool MacCool exterior.

Big Yin laughs sarcastically.

KING COOL
I warned you, lay one finger on her and...

BIG YIN
And just you remember MacCool - her fate is in your hands... So don't be a naughty boy... Now clear off!

KING COOL
I'll see you at first light in the morning, just make sure the Queen is with you.

King Cool stares lovingly at Queen Suraya and departs back to his headquarters. Big Yin turns to Queen Suraya.

BIG YIN
Now my dear! What are we going to do with you for the next few hours?

QUEEN SURAYA
Well, to start with, how's about a nice cup of tea.

SOBY
(Trying to sound polite and well-mannered)
Oh yes, Daddy, a wee cupa tae sounds like a great idea - my gob's absolutely parched!

Big Yin raises his eyebrows and looks with despair at SOBY.

BIG YIN
Very well, a nice cupa tae it is - after you, Your Majesty.

FADE TO BLACK.

EXT. GREAT CAUSEWAY - MIDNIGHT

Across the Causeway a flash of lightning picks up the silhouettes of four guards, - two of Big Yin's Stormtroopers and two Guardians. They are patrolling up and down below the prisoners Hugh and the President. CAMERA pans up to show the outline of both prisoners asleep and motionless. Down below we hear some scuffling sounds and muffled voices. More lightening flashes overhead and then we see only two Guardians on patrol. A few minutes later they are joined again by two of Big Yin's Stormtroopers. CAMERA tracks towards the two Stormtroopers. Surprisingly however, we hear familiar voices speaking softly from within the full-face visors and helmets of Big Yin's Stormtrooper Guards. One guard looks very large with a uniform that seems to be too small for him. King Cool and the President have now disguised themselves in the Stormtrooper Guards uniforms. One of the two Guardians watching over the prisoners is Conor.

KING COOL
(Whispers from within the visor)
Well done Conor, so far so good.

CONOR
(Whispers)
Aye ...it was handy that Big Yin's two guards decided to have a wee rest just now... so we'll not be hearing from them for a while... if you know what I mean!

PRESIDENT
(Trying to put on a Scottish accent)
But hopefully, You'll be hearing from us very soon laddie... with the biggest sound and light show this Causeway has ever seen.

CONOR
(Who is surprised to hear the President's voice)
But... but I thought... wait a minute... if you're down here...

He points up to the two prisoners.

CONOR
Who's that up there?

KING COOL
Watch out... they're coming to change the guards ...we'll explain all later!

CONOR
Oh right... good luck to you both - we're all depending on you - may God be with you.

Two new Stormtrooper Guards from Big Yin arrive to replace the Guards that King Cool and the President are now disguised as. There are more lightning flashes and thunder. King Cool and the President then walk towards Big Yin's troops. They are silhouetted in the lightning flashes. As they walk past, a half-sleeping Stormtrooper looks bemused at their contrast in size. The President speaks to him.

PRESIDENT
(In his Scottish accent)
All right pal! - ne bather!

The captain of Big Yin's guards is seen to approach King Cool and the President and speaks to them. King Cool tries to crouch low to make himself look small.

CAPTAIN
OK you two - get some shut eye...

(He looks quizzically at them)

You look as if you need it.

The two figures are seen to disappear among the rows of Big Yin's troops who are sleeping all over the Causeway. Various soldiers grumble and mutter in disapproval as King Cool and the President step on them as they make their way along the Causeway.

PRESIDENT
Sorry pal... there there now, go to sleep...
I'm just going for a leak.

KING COOL
(Whispers to the President)
What do you want a vegetable for at a time like this?

The President looks at King Cool with surprise, is about to make a comment, then changes his mind.

PRESIDENT
Forget it, I'll explain later.

King Cool and the President continue to make their way through the sleeping ranks of Big Yin's advance troops. They pass through the arches at the base of the imposing 19th Tower and on to the open causeway beyond. Eventually they reach the end of the sleeping Stormtroopers and find a clear area of the Causeway. Twinkling lights outline the vast extent of Big Yin's main army along the distant shore at the far end of the Causeway. King Cool begins to take out rolls and rolls of copper wire from within his uniform. The President looks bemused at the amount of stuff King Cool is unearthing from under his tunic.

PRESIDENT
You wouldn't have an oxyacetylene welder in there as well soldier?

KING COOL
Come on, let's get this fixed up. Over to you professor.

The President starts to fix the wire across the Causeway to create the outline of a large wire structure.

FADE TO BLACK.

EXT. ON THE GREAT CAUSEWAY - NIGHT

Fade up the sound of thunder. Pic fades up on a dramatic lightning flash as it illuminates the scene where King Cool and the President have erected a large wire pyramid shape across the full width of the Causeway.

A senior officer in Big Yin's Stormtroopers approaches them at the large pyramid structure. The President and King Cool look apprehensively at each other.

PRESIDENT
Oh sugar! Here comes trouble!

SENIOR STORMTROOPER
And what do you two think you're up to?

PRESIDENT
(In Scottish accent)
Shh! Quiet - special orders from Big Yin.
He wants to make a sort of marquee thing
for the trial - we're expecting a wee dram
o'rain ye see!

SENIOR STORM TROOPER
I did'ne hear anything about this!

PRESIDENT
No... it's very hush hush... I think Big Yin
has a bit of a plan... If you know what I
mean.

SENIOR GUARD
OK, but keep the noise down. These lads
want to sleep.

Senior Stormtrooper walks back towards the 19th Tower.

PRESIDENT
But... with a bit o' luck... they'll soon be
getting a very early alarm call... as long as
my High School physics experiment comes
up trumps.

King Cool finishes off forming the pyramid and points it into the sky. He brings a roll of wire attached to the pyramid structure back to the President.

KING COOL
There, that's the last of it.

PRESIDENT
Let's get out of here Finn... and pray that
we can whip up the biggest ever lightning
storm...
(MORE)

PRESIDENT (cont'd)
to give us a show that looks like it's the 4th of July, Chinese New Year, Diwali, Saint Patrick's Day, and Hogmanay all rolled into one... Here goes!

The President connects the last of the wires together and then they both make a rapid exit back through the Stormtroopers and towards the 19th Tower.

FADE TO BLACK.

INT. UPPER ROOM 19TH TOWER - NIGHT

Big Yin and SOBY are sitting together with Queen Suraya in an upper room of the 19th Tower. Big Yin is looking at Queen Suraya.

BIG YIN
You know you really are a very beautiful looking woman... for a Queen that is.

QUEEN SURAYA
Why thank you Big Yin for that surprise compliment... it seems somehow out of character. But then I don't really know you as a person... just your reputation. I'm sure you have a very beautiful Queen back home in your castle.

Big Yin looks over at the fat ugly face of SOBY.

BIG YIN
Well, let me put it this way... my Queen... SOBY's mother... her beauty is revealed in somewhat... unusual ways.

QUEEN SURAYA
My... you are a very fortunate man then... and you also have a fine strappin' big son in SOBY... So why this reputation for fighting, cruelty, treachery, thieving and sadistic brutality?

BIG YIN
I guess I'm just a lucky kind of a guy.

SOBY
But let me tell you this boy! ... My Da works very hard at being an evil despot.

QUEEN SURAYA
I'm sure he does... reputations like his don't just happen without a lot of hard work.

SOBY
Exactly!!

QUEEN SURAYA
Surely all that torture and killing must take a lot out of you... Do you ever think of taking it easy for a bit?... You know, relax... invent golf... or spend some time at home with the family.

BIG YIN
You are not only a beautiful woman... but you're funny as well. Yes, you have a very funny, sick sense of humour... which I must say... I like. I like your beautiful, funny, sick sense of humour... and you are also...

Big Yin starts to get angry.

BIG YIN
Very, very stupid at the same time!!

QUEEN SURAYA
Stupid???

BIG YIN
(Getting more angry)
Yes, very, very stupid... What do you mean... take a break, relax, spend time with the kids... Don't you know that maintaining my position as a barbaric villain is a 24/7 occupation... This is not one of your cosy Civil Service jobs, you know.

SOBY

Exactly!

QUEEN SURAYA

I'm sorry Big Yin, I didn't realize it was that hard... I thought it just came naturally to you. But you should think about it you know... after all, look what kind of an example you're setting for SOBY here.

BIG YIN

(He calms down a bit)

Woh... stop right now!... I can see what you're up to. Think you're very clever... can undermine the confidence of me and ma boy... That's it, I'm off to get some kip, I need me rest... I've got an awful lot of killin' to do tomorrow.

Big Yin gets up, and drags SOBY with him. As they go out they slam the door behind them. As the door slams closed there is a great flashing white light followed by a loud explosion.

INT. CORRIDOR OUTSIDE THE QUEEN'S ROOM, 19TH TOWER - NIGHT

BIG YIN

What the blazes is that?

They quickly open the door again to see the Queen lying on the floor. Big Yin shouts at the Queen.

BIG YIN

Just stay there and shut up... till I find out what's happening!

He quickly locks the door and leaves.

FADE TO BLACK.

Fighting Talk

13

EXT. THE GREAT CAUSEWAY - NIGHT

Suddenly the sky overhead lights up when a huge lightning bolt strikes onto the surface of the Causeway through the wire pyramid structure. It is followed by a succession of rapid lightning bolts. The surface of the Causeway is seen to start breaking up and the walls of the Causeway begin to fall into the sea. Big Yin's Stormtroopers wake up with startled screaming. Some are thrown into the air by the lightning strikes and they fall into the sea. Most try to run away from the area of the lightning strikes. They clamber over each other in panic.

The President and King Cool are caught up with Big Yin's Stormtroopers trying to escape. The rest of the troops on both sides are seen to waken up. The President and King Cool make it to the 19th Tower where they see Big Yin with SOBY and some of his Stormtroopers running ahead of them towards the place where the bodies of Hugh and the President are suspended on the side of the Causeway. The outline figures of the prisoners are still perched precariously over the parapet. The President and King Cool follow Big Yin and SOBY who are running towards the prisoners.

BIG YIN
What's going on?! Are we under attack?

COMMANDER OF BIG YIN'S STORMTROOPERS
Great leader... the Causeway behind us has been struck by a lightning attack, the whole expanse is crumbling into the sea, and we're now cut off from our main support army.

SOBY
Holy smoke! ...It looks like God has got really miffed after all. You know we should never have taken over the 19th Tower... it has always been forbidden.

They arrive puffing and out of breath beside the place where the President and Hugh are thought to be suspended.

BIG YIN

That's total crap... you sniffling wimp... You need look no further than our two alien visitors here for all this trouble... It's time to eliminate them once and for all.

Big Yin draws his sword and rushes towards the parapet with the rope holding up the President and Hugh. Guardians try to stop him but he just brushes them aside. CAMERA cuts to close up of the President and King Cool.

PRESIDENT

This wasn't meant to happen! We've got to stop him!

Big Yin rushes towards the rope and with one huge swing of his sword slices the rope in two. We see two bodies drop off the parapet and into the raging sea below. The President and King Cool arrive just at this point. The President sees what has happened and screams out!

PRESIDENT

Hugh... nooooh!!...

Big Yin turns round and looks towards King Cool and the President, he suddenly realizes who they are.

BIG YIN

Oops!!... Guess you're just too late.

PRESIDENT

You'll pay for this, believe me.

A group of Big Yin's Stormtroopers surround King Cool and the President, who are still dressed as Stormtroopers.

BIG YIN

You're in no position to threaten anyone... and by the way... it is an offence to impersonate one of my officers... which is punishable by death!! ... You'll not escape this time alien... And I believe it is time to finish you off for good, as well MacCool.

KING COOL
Come on Baz, it's too late to think about Hugh. Let me try to save you... come on, follow me.

King Cool with one mighty shove scatters all of the Stormtroopers surrounding them like bowling pins. King Cool and the President run towards the 19th Tower with Big Yin and SOBY in hot pursuit. They arrive at the great entrance of the 19th Tower.

Using his mighty golden sword, King Cool, followed by the President, fight off Stormtroopers as they run through the corridors of the 19th Tower. The Guardians start to attack Big Yin's forces and fight their way towards the 19th Tower. A full scale battle takes place between the two armies. King Cool and the President make their way down the steps under the 19th Tower.

INT. INSIDE THE 19TH TOWER - NIGHT

PRESIDENT
(Looking very distressed)
I should never have left Hugh!

KING COOL
All is destined, come on... we must ensure your return... this way, quickly.

King Cool and the President run through a maze of underground tunnels until they suddenly break through a large door and enter an enormous inner chamber with a stunning translucent golden light coming from one end. They both stop in their tracks as they are amazed by the wonder and awesome beauty of the shimmering light. Suddenly, the sound of Big Yin and SOBY can be heard running through the corridors after them. King Cool drags the President towards the great light, they stop in front of it.

INT. INNER CHAMBER OF THE GREAT ORB OF LIGHT - NIGHT

KING COOL
Time for us to say our good-byes
Mr. President - your future lies through there -
(MORE)

KING COOL (cont'd)
(He gestures towards the glistening orb of golden light)
...my destiny is to stay here, to prevent Big Yin and SOBY ...killing you!

Suddenly, Big Yin and SOBY enter the chamber. The four confront each other face to face.

PRESIDENT
No way Finn! The two of us can take them on - they're only a couple of big sissies.

SOBY snarls in anger at the President.

SOBY
I thought you were deed already... but you've saved me the personal delight in killing you ma self!

Big Yin stares at King Cool.

BIG YIN
And I've been waiting for this moment a long time MacCool. ...So it'll be a double delight of death.

KING COOL
Baz... all for one and one for all!

PRESIDENT
That's the spirit... King Finn MacCool.

The President reaches out his hand to shake King Cool's hand in a gesture of 'buddies together'. King Cool grasps his hand, but then surprisingly grabs hold of his back with his other hand and lifts the President off the ground. However, to do this he must let go of his sword, which drops precariously close to the edge of the platform they are standing on.

KING COOL
But this time... we'll do it in our separate ways. It's more important that you fulfill your destiny in 'your world' Mr. President.

The President is dangling in mid air.

PRESIDENT
Bu... but... Finn... what are you doing?!

KING COOL
In this world Baz, I make the decisions...
God speed my friend - our spirits will live
together forever!

He then throws the President into the great light at the centre of the Golden Orb. The President disappears and his voice is heard to scream as if falling through a time-travel tunnel.

PRESIDENT
Ahaaaah!!!!!!!!

King Cool turns back to confront Big Yin and SOBY, but as he does, his sword topples off the platform. He is defenceless. Big Yin and SOBY smile wryly at each other.

SOBY
Looks like your luck just ran out MacCool.

SOBY runs at King Cool followed by Big Yin. As SOBY lunges at King Cool with his sword, King Cool ducks down and throws SOBY over his back and he disappears into the centre of the Great Light. King Cool very quickly turns and thrusts his arm into the Great Light. We see part of King Cool's arm disappear. Big Yin by this time, is running sword in hand towards King Cool to kill him. However, just as Big Yin is about to strike King Cool, we see King Cool retrieve SOBY back through the Great Light by the scruff of the neck. King Cool hurls SOBY through the air towards Big Yin. They collide and fall like skittles on the ground. This gives King Cool time to jump down off the platform, retrieve his sword and once again stand in the path of Big Yin and SOBY.

KING COOL
(In calm and 'cool' tone)
All right you two, it's time you were taught
a few manners.

King Cool begins a high action sword fight with Big Yin and SOBY. They are joined by troops from both sides in a dramatic fight scene in the Great Chamber. After exchanging many blows with Big Yin and SOBY a stalemate begins to develop. King Cool starts talking to Big Yin and SOBY in his calm and 'cool' demeanor as they exchange blows.

KING COOL
You never did quite get it, you two... did you?

BIG YIN
No, but you're goin'a get what's bin comin' til ye for a long time!

Clangs and clinks of swords flashing intersperse with dialogue.

KING COOL
Tell me Big Yin - where has all your aggression and violence ever got you?... Man dear, you'd fight with your own shadow.

More sword clashes.

BIG YIN
I'm a fightin' man, I'll keep what's mine, that's the way men do it.

KING COOL
That's the way men used to do it... Some people are starting to learn, that to live together without violence, is the only way for true men and women to behave - just as the inner voice of the Great Light here has always told us! ...But no... you lead a people who are too stupid and selfish to listen. But where has it got you - what sort of a life do you have?

Big Yin stops fighting, becomes more subdued and speaks to King Cool.

BIG YIN
Even if I wanted - I can't stop!

KING COOL
Why not?

BIG YIN
You know why... I have my instructions! I must comply ...or be destroyed by that all controlling force of darkness...
(MORE)

BIG YIN (cont'd)
that Master of all oppression and evil - whose orders I must obey! ...And those orders were to stop those foreigners returning to their world. ...I've now failed to do that... so you know what happens to you... when you fail to obey the Dark force!

KING COOL
Yeh - absolutely nothing!

SOBY
Don't be daft man - you obviously haven't experienced the devious powers of sadistic cruelty that can be unleashed by the Lord of all Darkness.

KING COOL
That's where you are wrong... I have seen what that evil force calls power. However, evil becomes totally powerless when confronted by the truth and the courage to defend the virtues proclaimed through this pure light... by our Almighty Creator. The evil force just preys on your fears and your own selfish desires. Free yourself from these hypnotising threats... because evil depends on human weakness to do its foul and dirty deeds

(King Cool looks and points towards the eye of the great light behind him.)

You and your people can be free... when you all realize that the ways of evil are no match for the eternal power of the Great Spirit of Light - So that's why you can never get past me... even if we should stand here and fight for all eternity. I'll kill you both if I have to, but I don't want to - for it would only keep this feud going on and on between our peoples. Violence gets you nowhere - there is a better way.

King Cool turns to SOBY.

KING COOL
SOBY you've been to visit us - what did you think of our way of life?

SOBY stands and thinks for a minute - then turns to Big Yin.

SOBY
Aye right enough Da, when you come to think of it... that's a very nice place MacCool's got there... not like our dark and dreary...

Big Yin suddenly butts in, and starts fighting again.

BIG YIN
Dark and dreary, you thankless eejit don't listen to this con man, he'll turn your heed we' lies and nonsense.

SOBY
But it's not lies - I saw it for me self Da.

KING COOL
What sort of a father are you Big Yin? You teach your children only one thing and they grow up just like you - a big thug.

Big Yin looks towards his son. They are all exhausted with fighting and take deep breathes. Big Yin speaks in a more controlled and restrained voice.

BIG YIN
I fight because it's all I've ever known - it's the way I was taught - to look after me own.

KING COOL
I look after my own Big Yin... but I do it by looking after others!... It's a strange idea to get used to - but do you know, it works!
(MORE)

KING COOL (cont'd)
Why don't you and your boy come and stay with us for a while and let me show you...

Big Yin looks at his son.

KING COOL
And if you don't like it... sure we can come back here... and start fightin' again!

They begin to smile at each other.

SOBY
Sure we've nothin' to loose Da.

BIG YIN
If I'm honest, I'm gettin' tired of all this fightin'... maybe a break would do me good.

KING COOL
That's the spirit.

King Cool throws down his sword as a gesture of goodwill. SOBY then throws his sword down and eventually Big Yin also throws his sword down. The three giants turn and walk together through the Great Chamber. On the way out they shout at the soldiers to stop fighting.

INT. A CORRIDOR IN THE 19TH TOWER - DAYBREAK

BIG YIN
I think we have something of yours that we have to return MacCool.

KING COOL
That would be much appreciated.

FADE TO BLACK.

Pic fades up on King Cool, Big Yin and SOBY walking towards the room where the Queen is locked up. Outside the room King Cool steps forward and speaks.

INT. OUTSIDE THE QUEEN'S ROOM 19TH TOWER - MORNING

KING COOL
Let me do this, it will be a rather unexpected surprise.

King Cool approaches the door, unlocks it and is about to enter the room when SOBY shouts out.

SOBY
That's it... time to give her a nice big surprise!

As King Cool enters the dimly lit room, he suddenly catches a glimpse of the Queen running towards him. She is screaming and thrusting a large pointed spear aimed at his head. In a flash he moves his head just enough to miss his face but the spear catches his long golden hair and thuds into the large wooden door trapping King Cool against it. King Cool and the Queen scream out at the same time.

KING COOL
Ahaaaah!!

QUEEN SURAYA
Ahaaaah!!

When the Queen realizes that it is King Cool, she screams out again.

QUEEN SURAYA
(Panicked and breathless)
Oh my Heavens... it's you Finn... aaaahh!
...I almost killed you...

The Queen falls to the ground and starts crying. King Cool tries to remain cool.

KING COOL
It's OK... no major harm done... But excuse me my love, could you help me... I've got a little hair-spear here! - I think I may have some split ends!

The Queen gets up immediately but, still sobbing, hugs King Cool very tightly.

QUEEN SURAYA
Oh Finn! ...You're alive... and I almost killed you! ... But I don't understand... I just heard SOBY's voice outside the door...

King Cool is still pinned to the door.

KING COOL
The hair... the hair my love!!

The Queen starts to dislodge the spear from the door.

QUEEN SURAYA
Oh sorry my King... but what are the Big Yins doing here ... and why are <u>they</u> not killing you?!

KING COOL
Well, we've had a bit of a chat... and they've decided to come and stay with us for a while at our place.

QUEEN SURAYA
Honestly Finn... you never fail to amaze me... but this... this is special. Even by your standards Finn MacCool... you can talk your way around anybody - I guess that's why I love you so much...

KING COOL
I call it consulting... simple, honest consulting.

The Queen finally removes the spear from the door to free King Cool. She then amorously takes hold of King Cool's face and pushes him against the door. The two embrace in a long loving kiss.

Their loving encounter is suddenly disrupted when the door that the Queen and King Cool were leaning against is abruptly pushed open. They are both thrown to the floor by the force of the door opening and fall in a compromising position on the floor. SOBY enters and sees the Queen lying on top of King Cool.

SOBY

Oh! ...Very sorry there pal... I hope I'm not interrupting anything you know... I'm just checking that you're OK like... I don't want anything to happen to my new pal and his missus.

SOBY moves over and helps King Cool and the Queen up off the floor.

KING COOL

That's very kind of you SOBY... you know deep down you're really a very nice big lad... Come on, let's go home and we'll have a feast to celebrate our new friendship.

King Cool, the Queen, Big Yin and SOBY all walk off together down a corridor. We hear SOBY speak to the Queen as their voices fade off into the distance.

SOBY

You know I think the answer lies in parenting. ...Providing the proper early conditioning experiences is so important...

FADE TO BLACK.

EXT. 19TH TOWER - MORNING

Side by side, King Cool, the Queen, Big Yin and SOBY walk outside the 19th tower. All the soldiers from both sides begin to cheer and wave. Music swells into a happy shared victory scene with the soldiers from both sides.

DISSOLVE TO:

EXT. ENTRANCE TO THE GREAT CAUSEWAY - AFTERNOON

Pic opens on big celebration scene where King Cool, the Queen, Big Yin and SOBY return to King Cool's kingdom at the entrance to the Great Causeway. They smile and wave at the crowds of happy people who cheer and throw flowers over them. The ranks of Guardians and Stormtroopers are now happily chatting together as they are welcomed back. People begin to sing and dance to the infectious rhythmic beats of the King Cool theme song.

FADE TO BLACK.

Bridge of Harmony

14

ACT 3.

EXT. SEA - DAWN

Music fades up - sad, melancholy tone. Pic fades up on misty seascape. CAMERA tracks in on gently rippling waves. Outline of a figure floating face down in the water drifts into shot. CAMERA tracks down to reveal the distinctive outline of the President. He is motionless, partially lying on a piece of driftwood. Faint lights twinkle on a distant shoreline. CAMERA tracks towards the President's face. Then suddenly his nose twitches and his eyes slowly begin to open. CAMERA pulls back slowly as he begins to raise himself up on the driftwood. He rubs his eyes and as they begin to refocus, two giant-like figures are slowly revealed standing before him. At first he thinks they are more giants from the land of King Cool. He quietly talks to himself.

PRESIDENT

Oh no! For a moment there I thought this was all just a dream... But I must admit ...it feels very real ... not to mention very cold and very, very wet!

The President looks up again at the giant figures and then looks down into the water.

PRESIDENT

OK... just think this one out Baz... Number one - I'm wet and freezing. Number two - I am floating in an ocean somewhere in front of two huge giants ...and number three - somehow this doesn't feel like a dream.

(He thinks)

I'll just use some King Cool banter with them... warm and friendly like... maybe they know what's happened to King Finn.

The President looks up at the giant figures and speaks to them.

PRESIDENT
Hello there... how you doin'... perhaps you can help me. I wonder if you could please point me in the direction of King MacCool's castle?

The figures remain motionless, the President asks again.

PRESIDENT
You know... King Finn - the big cool guy... sure all you people know him.... Oh boy! What a man - God he's taught me a lot ...my life will never be the same.

The figures still don't move. The President talks to himself as he rubs his eyes again and looks up.

PRESIDENT
The reason why they are not saying anything Baz... is because these big giants are actually great big statues.

The statues seem to look down at him. Suddenly he hears a voice shouting above him.

JOGGER 1
Look there's somebody down there in the water!!

The President looks up to see two joggers looking down at him from a bridge between the two giant statues. The joggers wave at him. He waves back and then shouts at them.

PRESIDENT
Hi there... OK... by the way

(He then screams)

H..E..L..P!... HELP!!

JOGGER 2
Hold on... we'll get help!

The joggers rush to get help.

FADE TO BLACK.

Pic fades up to reveal the President sitting on a roadside bench, overlooking a bridge which is flanked on both sides by two large statues - one male and one female, made out of stone. The President is wrapped in a blanket, sipping a warm drink, surrounded by ambulance medics and police. The flashing lights of rescue vehicles flicker in the background. Press and TV cameramen hustle in to take pictures. The President poses for the cameras. A TV News journalist asks him a question.

EXT. ON A ROAD BESIDE THE BRIDGE OF THE GIANT STATUES - EARLY MORNING

TV JOURNALIST
President Obanna... this is totally amazing! What has happened to you?... We and the rest of the world all thought you had drowned!

Another journalist interrupts.

PRESS JOURNALIST
And how come you disappear at the Giant's Causeway... and turn up three days later in Carlingford Lough, over 100 miles away?... It's just unbelievable!

The President suddenly gets very animated.

PRESIDENT
Unbelievable! Unbelievable!! ... Let me tell you about unbelievable... Do you know...

Suddenly he stops in mid-sentence. He realizes that he cannot say to the media what has happened to him, otherwise they'll think he has lost his sanity. He then continues in a more calm and collected demeanor.

PRESIDENT
Do you know... I'm really glad to be here!

He smiles and the people around laugh with a sense of relief.

PRESIDENT

I'm sorry... at this moment it's all very vague, I guess I must have got a bump on the head or something.

(He chuckles)

And when I woke up and found myself floating in the water... I looked up and saw these rather large people here...

(He looks up at the statues)

I tell you... I thought I was in the land of the giants!!

Everyone laughs.

TV JOURNALIST

Like Finn MacCool!

PRESIDENT

The very man himself.

The newsman points towards a distant mountain.

TV JOURNALIST

Well you've come to the right place.

PRESIDENT

I have?

TV JOURNALIST

Oh yes, if you just look over there ...the locals around here know that as Cooley Mountain. They say when you look at its profile from a certain angle, you can see Finn MacCool himself ...takin' a nap.

PRESIDENT

So that's where he disappeared to... good old Finn... what a man!... How is he these days?... And all the MacCools, how are they all?

(MORE)

PRESIDENT (cont'd)
(He laughs, then his tone turns quite concerned and sombre).

Tell me, to be serious for a moment... does anyone know what happened to my friend Hugh MacCool who was with me at the Giant's Causeway?... And could someone lend me a phone... I need to speak to my wife urgently... God, what must she be thinking?!

All the people go quiet.

POLICEMAN 1
I'm afraid there's been no sign of Hugh MacCool anywhere Sir... Air-sea rescue, and the coast-guards have been searching the North Channel and the Irish Sea this past three days... We thought you both were lost.

PRESIDENT
(Looking very despondent a tear comes to his eye)
Poor old Hugh - God, he was a lovely man...
(He swallows hard)

The President then breaks down. The people around try to comfort him. The President, tearful, looks up at the statues on the bridge.

PRESIDENT
Even they look sad...

Pic cuts to a close up of the face on one of the statues.

PRESIDENT
Who are these statues anyway?

Pic cuts to a wide shot of the bridge and the surrounding green fields.

PRESS JOURNALIST

This is our 'Bridge of Harmony' ...it joins Ireland and Northern Ireland at the 'Narrow Waters' of Carlingford Lough.

Pic cuts back to TV journalist.

TV JOURNALIST

The bridge is a symbolic beacon for people throughout Ireland, and was built to show that by working together in peace and unity... it is a much better way for us all to live.

PRESS JOURNALIST

In a community that has been divided and at war for hundreds of years... it's been a hard lesson for us all to learn.

PRESIDENT

(In a more serious tone)

It's a lesson that the whole world is finding difficult to learn...

(He looks up at the statue again)

They should be an inspiration for everyone, in every land... just as your bravery to rescue me and kindness to look after me... will be forever etched in my heart. Thank you all. I'll never forget you...

The President looks around at the sun rising over the bay.

PRESIDENT

Nor will I ever forget my experiences here in this wonderful and beautiful land.

He looks into the distance. A policeman interrupts his gaze and hands the President a mobile phone. He walks out of shot in conversation on the phone.

FADE TO BLACK.

White House Blues

15

Fade up on the exterior of the White House in Washington DC. Mix to pic of the Oval office where the President is reunited with Ruben his election agent and personal staff George and Lucy. The President is sitting behind his desk somewhat distant and deep in his thoughts. Ruben speaks to the President.

INT. THE OVAL OFFICE, THE WHITE HOUSE, WASHINGTON DC - MORNING

RUBEN
Mr. President... can I say something?

PRESIDENT
(In a distant tone)
Oh! Ah... yea... shoot.

RUBEN
With all the publicity you've received world-wide after your unbelievable rescue from the Irish Sea, your opinion poll ratings are the highest ever. If you were popular before - they're now calling you 'The Miracle Man' - it's like you're some sort of a God. They're saying there's no need to hold an election - they've stopped taking bets on the outcome... It appears you're a shoe-in for another four year term... congratulations!

He stops, gets up and walks over to face the President at his desk.

RUBEN
But if you don't mind me saying... you don't exactly look like a President who is euphoric about winning a second term in office.

The President is quiet and calmly looks up at Ruben. He is quite humble.

PRESIDENT
I'm sorry Ruben, I don't feel very euphoric at present... I don't feel very much of anything to be honest. There was a time when all I could think about was winning a second term... Now... I'm not so sure!

LUCY
You've changed a lot since you came back from Ireland Mr. President.

PRESIDENT
Yea, isn't that ironic... there I was seeking to bring change to the world... I go and visit Ireland... and it changes me.

(He sighs deeply)

No news yet about Hugh MacCool?

GEORGE
Nothing Mr. President. But I understand they are continuing the search.

PRESIDENT
Poor old Hugh... I only knew him a short while... but I really got very attached to him.

The President breaks down again. Ruben goes over to comfort him and quietly speaks to him one-to-one as a friend.

RUBEN
Baz, I know this has all been very difficult for you to deal with... but this is not the time to let it all slip. The only way you can loose this election now... is if you screw it up yourself.

The President looks even more depressed and despondent. Ruben stands back from the President and openly addresses everyone in the room.

RUBEN
Mr. President... there are a lot of issues that need some answers... and quite a few people who need to see you... So for the people of America... and your own well-being... you really need to snap out of this one.

Ruben turns and talks to Lucy, trying to bring some humour into a somewhat depressed mood.

RUBEN

Lucy, book him no more holidays, they just don't agree with him... come on Baz... you're going to have to face the real world sooner or later.

The President gets agitated and angry.

PRESIDENT

That's where you're wrong my friend, this is nothing like the real world... The real world is free, it's happy... and it's honest!

LUCY

How do you know?

PRESIDENT

I've been there!...

Suddenly he stops, calms down, and thinks for a moment to himself. He then continues.

PRESIDENT

I've been... oh... I've been... thinking... I really need to go and see my girls.

He gets up from his chair. On his way out of the room he quietly talks to Ruben.

PRESIDENT

I'm sorry Ruben, you're just going to have to give me a little more time to get this sorted out.

He walks out of the room.

FADE TO BLACK.

Fade up music with dramatic breaking news theme. Montage of pics showing newspaper headlines:

(1) "LANDSLIDE WIN FOR PRESIDENT OBANNA".

(2) "WORLD WELCOMES SECOND TERM VICTORY".

(3) "'BAZMANIA' TAKES OVER".

Newspaper headlines fade. Mix up exterior pic of the White House at night. Mix to interior pic where we find the President and the First Lady in their bedroom getting ready to go out to the post-election party to celebrate his second term victory. The President is lying across the bed looking distant and quiet. The First Lady sits at a dressing table.

INT. PRESIDENT'S BEDROOM - WHITE HOUSE, WASHINGTON DC - EVENING

FIRST LADY

For a man who's about to celebrate winning a second term as leader of the free world... you don't seem at all interested. Come on Baz... let's hear it... I know you've had a miraculous escape from death in Ireland... but I know you... something else happened to you at the Giant's Causeway!... I haven't pressed you on it... but even the girls keep saying to me - 'What's up with dad? - He's different'.

PRESIDENT

Is it bad different... or good different?

FIRST LADY

I don't know... it's just different.

She gets up and goes over to the President. She sits beside him on the bed and starts to stroke his head.

PRESIDENT

I'm sorry to do this to you and the girls... I don't mean to upset you... you know that.

FIRST LADY
I know... But I think it's time for us to talk. You have a big speech to make tonight and I just want you to be in the right frame of mind... that's all.

PRESIDENT
It's really hard to explain... but you're right... things did happen to me at the Giant's Causeway... strange things. So strange that if I really told you what happened... you might think that I have now completely flipped... following my near death experience...

The President sits up on the bed and suddenly becomes bright and enthused.

PRESIDENT
But I tell you Rachel... it was the most amazing experience I've ever had in my life... I'm not going to give you any details... All I can say is that this experience... has completely changed my view on life... my view on politics... and my view on the future.

FIRST LADY
What about your view on your family?

PRESIDENT
Oh hun... that's the one thing I'm absolutely crystal clear about. The importance of you and the children, now centres every thought I have... I've never felt so close and so much in love with you and the girls.

They kiss and embrace.

PRESIDENT
It's all the other stuff that bothers me. This job... the frustrations I come up against just trying to get things right.
(MORE)

PRESIDENT (cont'd)
Everyday you have to end up compromising your own beliefs so that the system just keeps running the way it always has. I try to keep a brave face on it in public... but beneath the surface... I'm getting more frustrated and more undecided about where my future truly lies.

FIRST LADY
Well if you don't mind me saying so Baz... you're cutting it a bit fine if you're considering a career change.

She looks at her watch.

FIRST LADY
I give you about forty five minutes... an hour at the outside.

They both laugh and embrace again.

PRESIDENT
I simply don't know what I'd do without you.

FIRST LADY
The important thing for you... the important thing for us... and the important thing for this country... is for you to do... what you feel in your heart... is the right thing to do. I don't exactly know what's going on in your head... or what you've seen or experienced... all I know is that I love you and I hate to see you like this. I know you have some very big decisions to make... but you know... whatever you decide I'm right there beside you.

They embrace affectionately. The President gets up, puts on his jacket and begins to sound much more upbeat and happy.

PRESIDENT
You know Rachel... I haven't been picking enough flowers for you and the girls.

The First Lady is somewhat surprised by this comment.

FIRST LADY
But we always have flowers in the White House.

The President starts to get very excited.

PRESIDENT
No... I mean real flower picking... going out into the countryside and picking real flowers... By the way... there's a very good song which accompanies flower picking... I'm going to teach it to you and the girls... Believe me, the effect it can have on the flowers is amazing.

The First Lady looks somewhat perplexed.

FIRST LADY
You... singing to flowers? ...This I gotta see!

They both laugh and leave the room. On the way out the President starts to hum the intro to the flowers 'Pick Me' song.

FADE TO BLACK.

Choose Your Future

16

INT. CONVENTION CENTRE - EVENING

Sound fades up with patriotic 'Stars and Stripes' music. Pic fades up on huge indoor stadium decked out for the post-election party with posters, balloons, flags and banners. Thousands of people are cheering and singing as the frenzied atmosphere builds. From the podium, the MC speaks to the audience to announce the arrival of the President. The crowd goes wild with excitement as the President, the First Lady and their two children enter the auditorium. They are led in procession through the arena to the main platform where the President receives a hero's welcome. Eventually he is introduced to the audience by the MC.

MC

Ladies and gentlemen... not that long ago our hopes for this great occasion were suddenly dashed... we thought this day would no longer happen. But we Americans have a saying - "It's hard to keep a good man down".

Audience laughs.

MC

Never before has that saying been so apt as it is here today... because I'm about to introduce to you, not just a good man - but a great man! ...A man, who like Lazarus, knows how to rise to the occasion... And the occasions don't get much bigger than this one... Ladies and gentlemen, it is my very great honour to welcome here tonight... our very special leader and President.

Audience cheers.

MC

...They talk about the 'Come-Back Kid'... well, there's never been a come-back like this... Because for this man, the impossible is not just possible... but probable. That's why I give you the man who has truly earned our respect and our votes... for his second term in office...

(MORE)

MC (cont'd)
Ladies and gentlemen... I give you the next President of the United States of America... President Abbas Obanna

Crowd goes wild, fanfares are sounded. The President waves to the audience and acknowledges the enthusiastic applause. He walks to the podium to address the audience. The crowd eventually settles. He speaks, but his tone is somewhat subdued.

PRESIDENT
My fellow Americans - thank you for this amazing reception. I'm really touched by your welcome and heart-felt concern... First of all I want to say how grateful I am... that God has spared me to stand before you today. When you've had a near-death experience... like I've just had during my visit to Ireland... you are suddenly confronted with reality. The reality that I now have to face... is not just in the short term over the next four years... but is, more importantly, over the long term. So recently I've been asking myself... in the long term... where do I want to spend eternity? ... My near death experience has led me to discover that there are in fact two Abbas Obannas... There's Abbas Obanna - who is the President of the United States of America... and there's Abbas Obanna - the private individual. I've now discovered that they are in fact... two very different people. I've discovered that if the man Abbas Obanna, wants to do something... then President Obanna... may not be able to go along with him. You see, I now realize that even the President of the United States... can't buck the system!... So, my near-death experience, has forced me to confront myself, to ask this question... the political system, that's in place at present - where is it really taking us?...

(MORE)

PRESIDENT (cont'd)
More wars, more financial crisis and corporate greed, more pandemic diseases and health-care wranglings, more poverty and jobs uncertainty - and more divisions in our political governance and throughout society as a whole. Just ask yourself - are the divisions created by a system of Party Politics... really proving to be the best way to take our country forward... for everyone's benefit?... I have tried as your President to bring change to solve many of these problems. I've discovered however that the current system won't let me. Now confronted by facing my own eternity... I feel I must now spend my time searching out a better way forward... and to find out if there is perhaps a different system that can produce fair governance for all. Governance, where freedom and real democracy... equality, unity and harmony... can truly be established... not just for the people of America... but for every citizen in the world. I believe a new and better system is out there... it's just somehow got hidden... and together, we can find that new way forward... together, we can create real change for the betterment of all humanity... My near-death experience has forced me to be honest... I must be honest to myself... but most of all... I must be honest with you... the great American people. So that is why I have made this decision just today - following much heartfelt and honest consultation with myself and my family... Tonight I must inform you... that I have to decline accepting a second term as your President!

Audience suddenly hush. A gasp of disbelief surges across the arena... media journalists look up in astonishment.

The audience begins to shout and then starts chanting and stamping their feet. No, no, Obanna for President... Obanna for President! CAMERA goes to a close up of the First Lady, Ruben, George, Lucy, etc. All look in a state of shock. Eventually the President brings about some order.

PRESIDENT
Ladies and gentlemen...

The President lets out a deep sigh of relief. He begins to sound more upbeat and enthusiastic.

PRESIDENT
Wow! ...By just getting that all off my chest... I can tell you... as the man Abbas Obanna... my heart now feels exhilarated and free. I'm excited about the road ahead... and believe we can now bring real change... with a new way and a new attitude. One that seeks to unite humanity, not divide it. I believe... that is what God wants us to do... and we can achieve it by discovering that new way forward... free from the corruption and inefficiencies of our old system... a system that I've had to try to deal with for the past four years... at all levels. When we find that new way forward... then I believe... that God will truly bless... not just America... but all nations around the world. Together... let us find that new way!

The crowd remains stunned and silent. CAMERA tracks in towards the First Lady and her two children. Eventually the young girls start to smile and clap their hands in approval. The First Lady, George, Lucy and Ruben then follow their lead and begin to applaud. Suddenly a ripple of applause starts to build among the audience and eventually turns into a crescendo of spontaneous applause and cheering.

Cut to close up of band leader who strikes up the band to play - 'For he's a jolly good fellow'. The First Lady and the girls rush up to the podium to greet the President. He hugs and kisses the girls then he looks at the First Lady. They smile at each other, then break into laughter.

They hug and kiss in a warm embrace. Ruben, George and Lucy join them at the podium. Ruben whispers to the President.

RUBEN

Baz... we had arranged a little surprise finale for you. However, you seem to be leading with all the surprises... but what the heck... under the circumstances - we may as well just go right ahead with it - Strike up the Band!

Suddenly there is a fanfare of music, audience noise fades, there are rhythmic drumbeats and the music changes to the King Cool theme song. From the back of the arena the audience is seen dividing to make a pathway up the centre of the arena. The crowd starts cheering as we see a group of people entering from the back of the arena carrying aloft on their shoulders - a man.

PRESIDENT

What's going on?!

FIRST LADY

Looks like you have a rival hero, Baz.

PRESIDENT

What the... !

Suddenly the President's face is frozen. On the large video screens around the arena, they show a close-up of a man's face. It is Hugh MacCool.

PRESIDENT

I don't... I don't understand!

He shakes his head in disbelief.

PRESIDENT

...It can't be...

Tears start to flow from the President's eyes.

PRESIDENT

...Oh God... it is!

Suddenly the President springs to life and jumps off the platform, and moves through the crowd towards Hugh. He starts shouting with excitement.

PRESIDENT
Hugh, my God Hugh!

Suddenly the President is lifted shoulder high by his supporters, who start to carry him in the direction of Hugh. King Cool theme music builds as the President and Hugh are carried closer. They both look at each other and smile. Hugh gives the President a friendly wave. Tears are still rolling down the President's face. At a climax of the music, still being held aloft above the crowd, they meet in the centre of the arena and are greeted with a huge roar of the crowd. As if in a world of their own they embrace each other.

PRESIDENT
(Sounding amazed and excited
tears rolling down his face)
I can't believe it, Hugh. You're alive. I just
can't believe it...

HUGH
(Being very cool and matter of
fact - Hugh style)
It's me alright Baz... sure they even gave
me a badge...

(He points down at a name
lapel badge on his jacket)

...This is to show like that it's officially me.

The President looks at the badge and pronounces it like 'Who MacCool'.

PRESIDENT
Hugh MacCool...

(Then he looks at Hugh)

Yes it's definitely you... Hugh.

(They laugh)

HUGH

You're right Baz... boy there's a quare amount of 'yo-whooin' goin' on here tonight.

PRESIDENT

No I'm definitely not going there again. ... But listen here Hugh, how did you get here?... I just don't understand...

The President gets closer to Hugh and whispers in his ear.

PRESIDENT

Hugh, I saw you being thrown off the Great Causeway into the poisoned seas with my own eyes.

HUGH

Ah no... you thought that's what you saw... but no... what you saw was something completely different.

PRESIDENT

Please, I don't understand, tell me.

HUGH

(Looking vaguely to the sky)

Oh boy, that King Finn MacCool, God he's a smart man.

PRESIDENT

He is the one and only... the original 'King of Cool'.

HUGH

Well you remember when we pretended that you were with me at the big gallows thing to fool Big Yin... but it wasn't you at all... it was a substitute made-up dummy.

PRESIDENT

...Yes.

HUGH

Well when you and Finn were creating all the thunder and lightning on the Causeway and diverting Big Yin's attention... Finn arranged for two of the Guardians to quickly run up, release me, and leave another dummy in my place as well... It was done in the blink of an eye... God he was great... Wasn't he Baz?

The President looks awestruck.

PRESIDENT

The most amazing person I've ever met...

(Then he thinks)

...after you that is Hugh.

They laugh and hug each other.

PRESIDENT

But Hugh how did you manage to get from there to here?

HUGH

Now there's another really good story and I'll tell you it later... But sure, it was all a great adventure we had Baz.

PRESIDENT

The real adventure is only about to begin Hugh, and I'd love us to share that dream together.

HUGH

You can count on me Baz!

PRESIDENT

(Once again whispers in Hugh's ear)

Hugh, have you sort of said anything to anybody about our experience... about Finn and the Great Causeway and all?

HUGH
Oh God no Baz... that's between you and me... sure if you told anybody the truth... they'd think we were a couple of nutters... and they'd lock us up and throw away the key.

PRESIDENT
Well, if you haven't said anything... how come I recognize a certain person's song playing at this moment in time.

HUGH
Ah well, ... I told them that was a song I taught you and you really liked it. So it would be a bit of a surprise for you tonight... sure they'll never know.

PRESIDENT
Hugh ...you really are unbelievable... I tell you, there's more than one... cool MacCool.

They both laugh as they are separated from each other by the jostling crowd. Hugh shouts to the President.

HUGH
This is great up here Baz, sure it's like we're a couple of big giants!

PRESIDENT
Now come on Hugh, you're letting your imagination get carried away...

They both smile at each other. CAMERA pulls back to show everyone in arena dancing and partying to the infectious rhythms of the King Cool music theme.

THE END.

So how will our destiny unfold?

Look out for some incredible revelations in Adam Goodman's amazing follow up story.... available soon!

www.goldenorbpublications.com

For more information and to keep up to date with the latest developments in the 'Cool World' go online to

www . kingcool . tv